Christ's Life in the Life of Christians

Christ's Life

in the Life of Christians

Grace Dola Balogun

Grace Religious Books Publishers & Distributing, Inc.

Library of Congress Control Number: 2013956552

Published by:
Grace Religious Books Publishing & Distributors, Inc.
213 Bennett Avenue
New York, NY, 10040

First Edition © 2013 by Grace Dola Balogun

Hardcover ISBN: 9781939415523
Softcover ISBN: 9781939415516

Cover Design by Lisa Hainline www.lisahainline.com

Printed in the United States of America
www.gracereligiousbookspublishers.com

"As the Father has loved me, so have I loved you. Now remain in my love. If you obey my commands, you will remain in my love, just as I have obeyed my Father's commands and remain in his love" (John 15:9-10).

Contents

Dedication

I DEDICATE THIS BOOK TO OUR GOD THE FATHER Almighty who spoke through His prophets in the Old Testament to our forefathers. At many times, in various ways, for various reasons, He communicated himself and his will to the men of the world. Jesus Christ is the begotten Son. He is the radiance of God's glory and the exact representation of his being. God is sustaining all things by his powerful word. Christ is God's word and wisdom incarnate. Christ is the attribute of God the Father, just as our words and thoughts come from us and cannot be separated from us, the same way Jesus Christ cannot be separated from the Father. Christ the heir of all things, by him, God made the worlds, visible and invisible, the heavens and the earth. He upholds all things by the word of his power. Christ is the glory of the Father, shining forth with a truly divine splendor; Jesus Christ is God manifest in the flesh. In beholding the power, wisdom and goodness of the Lord Jesus Christ, we behold the power and wisdom of the Father. Christ is the word of God, the speech of God, Christ the living word of God who lives forevermore. Christ is the wisdom of God and the power of God.

I also dedicate this book to those who will read it and acquire great wisdom and knowledge to read and believe that in Christ the righteousness of God is being revealed from faith to faith. They will live by faith to the point that they will give their lives to the one and only, the word of God and to God. To all the people on earth who seek their own wisdom, finally one day they will come to the knowledge and understanding of the wisdom of God in their lives. They will also know that Christ is the most excellent messenger who was ever sent by God the Father to the world; he is the full, final and the finishing revelation.

Preface

ESUS CHRIST IS THE LIFE OF ALL THOSE WHO IN HIM GAVE their life to him in humble obedience and faith as well as in total surrender to his will. Christ said, "I am the true vine, and my Father is the Gardner, he cuts off every branch in me that bears no fruit, while every branch that does bear fruit, he prunes so that it will be even more fruitful" (John 15:1-2). Jesus Christ is the vine of truth planted in the vineyard of all Christians. The vine is a spreading plant, as Jesus Christ will be known as the source of salvation and the gift of grace to all the people of the world.

Christians are the branches of the vine, which means Christ is the source of life of every Christian; he is also the root of the vine. The root of the tree diffuses sap to it and is all in all flourishing and bearing more and more fruits. In Christ, all Christians get support and supplies of all their needs. The branches cannot survive without the vine. Therefore, all Christians are all one in Christ no matter in what area of the world they are living; Christ is the bond and the center of Christian unity and lives. By remaining attached to Jesus Christ as the source of life, Christians produce fruits. God the Father is the gardener who takes care of the branches so that they may bear fruits. God expects all the Christian believers to bear fruits.

After a Christian believes in Jesus, he or she is forgiven. He or she receives the gift of grace and eternal life, and it gives the believer the power to remain in Christ. Receiving that power, Christians must resume the responsibility in salvation to remain in Christ, abide or live a life in Christ Jesus. Just as branches have life as long as the life of the vine flows into it. Christians have Christ's life only as long as Christ's life flows into the Christians through their remaining in Christ. Christ's love is Christian love, for he laid down his life for believers. He bought them with his precious blood on the cross.

All those who believe in Jesus Christ are the friends of Christ Jesus. Christ is the friend who loves at all times. Jesus Christ gave the believers all that he received from the Father; Jesus Christ baptized all Christians with the Holy Spirit. By keeping Christ's commandments, Christians will continue to grow in grace and grow in sanctification and in the end, they will live with Christ in his eternal glory in heaven forever.

The Scripture revealed, "Those who live according to the sinful nature have their minds set on what that nature desires, but those who live in accordance with the Spirit have their minds set on what the Spirit desires. The mind of sinful man is death, but the mind controlled by the Spirit is life and peace, the sinful mind is hostile to God. It does not submit to God's law, nor can it do so. Those controlled by the sinful nature cannot please God. You however, are controlled not by the sinful nature but by the Spirit. If the Spirit of God lives in you; and if anyone is without the Spirit of Christ he does not belong to Christ. But if Christ is in you, your body is dead because of sin, yet your spirit is alive because of righteousness" (Roman 8:5-10). Apostle Paul was telling believers that to live according to the sinful nature is to be occupied with its desires, thoughts, emotions and physical gratification. This includes sexual immorality, adultery, hatred, selfish ambitions, outbursts of anger and drug addiction. Whereby, if Christians live in accordance with the Spirit, they submit to the Holy Spirit's direction, control and enablement, and they focus their attention, thought, energy and values on God. At all times, their minds are in the presence of God, trusting him to give them the help and grace they may need to accomplish his will through the lives of Christians. The Spirit of Jesus Christ will live inside of believers. The Holy Spirit's empowerment and indwelling presence of the Lord will overflow from Christians to all others around them.

Apostle Paul stated in the Scripture, "I have been crucified with Christ; and I no longer live but Christ lives in me. The life I live in the body, I live by faith in the son of God, who loved me and gave himself for me" (Galatians 2:20). Apostle Paul describes his relationship with Christ in terms of a personal profound attachment to and reliance on his Lord, which should be the same for those who have faith in the Lord Jesus Christ today. Christians should live their lives in intimate union with the Lord, both in his death and resurrection.

Believers have been crucified with Christ on the cross. Christians have died to the law and received the blessing of salvation; they now live through Jesus Christ for God. Christians have been crucified with Christ and live with him in his resurrection life. Christians share in Christ's death. Resurrection is appropriated through faith. Christian's living by faith can be seen as living by the Spirit. The old man is crucified but the new man who lives in Christ; sin mortified and the grace of God is quickened in believers. The gift of grace has triumphs over sin. Christians die unto sinful lives by faith in Christ, which is higher than any other law of sin. All those who believe in Christ by faith must die unto sin, so that they can be able to receive Christ's life and live unto God. Believers live in the flesh and yet live by faith. Jesus Christ is the Christians' life.

Christians who are living in Jesus Christ's life allow the Holy Spirit who raised Jesus Christ from the dead to desire to impart the life of Jesus Christ into their mortal bodies as they embrace his life within them. Christians will automatically put to death the misdeeds of the flesh. The Holy Spirit, also known as the Spirit of Christ, lives within all the children of God in order to lead them to think, speak and act according to God's word.

"By faith Abraham, when called to go to a place he would later receive as his inheritance, obeyed and went, even though he did not know where he was going" (Hebrews 11:8). All the believing Christians in all the world must know that faith and obedience are inseparable, just as unbelief and disobedience are inseparable.

"Praise be to the God and Father of our Lord Jesus Christ, who has blessed us in the heavenly realms with every spiritual blessing in Christ. For he chose us in him before the creation of the world to be holy and blameless in his sight. In love he predestined us to be adopted as his sons through Jesus Christ, in accordance with his pleasure and will—to the praise of his glorious grace, which he has freely given us in the one he loves. In him we have redemption through his blood, the forgiveness f sins, in accordance with the riches of God's grace that he lavished on us with all wisdom and understanding" (Ephesians 1:3-7).

1

Jesus Christ is our Life

JESUS CHRIST IS OUR LIFE, THE LIFE OF ALL CHRISTIANS IN the world. Without the life of Jesus Christ in the Christian life, they will not be able to function as Christians, and they will not be able to have the power of the indwelling of the Holy Spirit. To make it clear and precise without Christ, Christians, called the body of Christ, will not be able to do anything and they will be nothing.

During Jesus Christ's earthly ministry, he said, "I am the vine, you are the branches. If a man remains in me and I in him, he will bear much fruit; apart from me you can do nothing. If anyone does not remain in me, he is like a branch that is thrown away and withers; such branches are picked up, thrown into the fire and burned" (John 15:5-6). In these words of Jesus, he was describing or telling all those who believed in him that he is the true vine; all those who followed him are like branches. We Christians became his disciples, his followers, his children, his servants, his messengers. We must remain attached, glued as the source of our life, in order to bear fruits. God the Father is the gardener who takes care of the branches so that we may continuously bear fruits in the garden of the Lord.

God, Almighty Father of all who believe in him, has set up the following requirements and he requires and expects from all the believers to bear fruits. Studying the Scripture, we determine that there are two categories of branches: (1) there are some branches that are fruitless, barren branches, and dry branches; and (2) there are branches that are fruitful, continuously bearing fruits in every area of their lives. The branches that are fruitless stop bearing fruit. They are those who no longer have the life in them, the life that comes from enduring faith and love for the Lord Jesus Christ. These fruitless branches the Father pruned or severed from the vine. The Father separates them from vital union with Christ.

John the Baptist was preaching about the non-bearing fruits before he was martyred by King Herod, "I tell you that out of these stones God can raise up children for Abraham. The ax is already at the root of the trees, and every tree that does not produce good fruit will be cut down and thrown into the fire" (Matthew 3:9b-10). John the Baptist was preaching about genuine repentance, which will be accompanied by the fruit of righteousness. In other words, true saving faith and conversion must become the evidence through lives that forsake sin and bear godly fruit.

There are many people in this world. According to the Scripture, they say they profess that they believe in Christ and are God's children; yet they still live lives of sin and wickedness to others. They are not producing good fruit for the kingdom of God. They are like a tree that will be cut down and thrown into the fire. Trees that stand and look the same but they are not the same, will be cut down because they are not bearing any fruit. These are the branches, the believers who stop remaining in Christ. They stop having life in Christ. They follow another God; therefore, the Father severed them and threw them into the fire.

The branches that are fruitful and bear fruits are those who have life in them because of their enduring love and faith in Jesus Christ. The fruit bearing branches the Father prunes so that they will be able to bear more and more fruits; they will become more fruitful in the kingdom of God, which means Christ Jesus will remove from their lives anything to the contrary that can divert their way, or mind, anything that can hinder the vital, ever-flowing life of Christ in their lives.

They will receive the qualities of Christian character that bring glory to their Lord and Savior throughout their lives and they will witness. "They will produce fruit in keeping with repentance" (Matthew 3:8). John the Baptist taught and preached that a good repentant heart will bear good fruit into the kingdom of God. John said that the work of the coming Messiah would be baptizing people with the Holy Spirit. "But now that you have been set free from sin and have become slaves to God, the benefit you reap leads to holiness and the result is eternal life" (Romans 6:20).

The Scripture teaches that after sinners believe in Jesus Christ and all his or her sins are forgiven, they receive eternal life and the power to remain in Christ with the power of the Holy Spirit bestowed upon them. They must accept the responsibility in salvation; they must remain in Christ. They must continue to abide in Christ or live in Christ. Just as the branches have life only as long as Christ's life flows into them and manifests into them through their remaining in Christ. Conditions that can help Christians to remain in Christ are as follows: Christians must keep God's word continually in their hearts and minds, spirits, souls, and bodies; and by making God's word the guidance of all their actions. Our Lord said,

"If you remain in me, and my words remain in you, ask whatever you wish and it will be given you" (John 15:7).

To remain in Christ, Christians must maintain the habit of constant intimate communion with Jesus Christ in order to draw strength from him. Our prayers form one of the strengths and where the strength will come from is through our prayers. The answer to our prayers will make Christians remain in Christ. In other words, the more intimate that our life in Christ is through prayer, fasting, worship and meditation on, and study of, the Scriptures, the more our prayers will be in line with the nature and words of Christ, and therefore, the more effectual our prayers will be.

The Lord said, "And I will do whatever you ask in my name, so that the Son may bring glory to the Father" (John14:13). Prayer will help Christians remain in Christ, as well as bear fruit into the kingdom. Prayer in Jesus' name involves two things: (1) prayer will help us to live in good harmony with Christ's nature, his character and to live according to his will; and (2) prayer will strengthen our faith in Christ and his authority; we will have a desire to glorify both God the Father and God the Son.

Our Beloved Apostle Peter answered people's questions, "By faith in the name of Jesus, this man whom you see and know was made strong. It is Jesus' name and faith that comes through him that has given this complete healing to him, as you can all see"(Acts 3:16). Believers must pray in the name of Jesus Christ, means that Jesus will answer any prayer that he would have prayed himself. There is no limit to the power of prayer when Christians direct it to Christ Jesus, or God the Father in holy faith according to his desire.

All those who believe in Jesus Christ will remain in him through effective communication of prayer in his holy name.

The disciples ask Jesus, "Then the disciples came to Jesus in private and asked; why couldn't we drive it out? He replied, because you have so little faith, I tell you the truth, if you have faith as small as a mustard seed, you can say to this mountain, move from here to there and it will move, nothing will be impossible for you" (Matthew 17:19-20). Our Lord Jesus Christ always talked about faith during his earthly ministry. He frequently comments on the nature of true faith. He teaches and speaks of a faith that can move mountains, faith that can bring miracles and healing, and a faith that can accomplish great things for God.

Jesus speaks about true faith, an effective faith that produces good results that can bring great changes to our lives that can move mountains and make wonderful things to happen in our lives, a faith in God that is true. True faith is the work of God the Father Almighty within the hearts of all Christians. True faith involves an awareness divinely imparted to believers' hearts that answer his or her prayers, the faith that the Holy Spirit created within us that we cannot produce on our own power. This true faith is imparted to all those who believe in Jesus Christ. It is very important to draw near, to remain in Jesus Christ and his word. Christians must deepen their commitment to Christ and have confidence in Jesus Christ. Christians must be dependent on Jesus Christ for everything they do or say. Therefore, Christians must make Jesus Christ the author and finisher of their faith.

Christ's close presence will be revealed in Christian lives and Christian obedience to his word is the source of strength and the secret of true faith. Christians will be able to remain in Christ and bear fruits if they obey his commands, remaining in his love continuously and loving each other. The Scripture says, As the Father has loved me, so have I loved you. Now remain in my love. If you obey my commands you will remain in my love, just as I have obeyed my Father's commands and remain in his love" (John 15:9-10).

The secret of answered to prayers is for Christian to remain in Christ. The more intimate that our life in Jesus Christ is through prayers, the happier we become. Jesus Christ gave believers a solemn and loving warning that it is possible for true believers to ultimately abandon faith and turn their backs on Jesus, fail to remain in him, and thus, to be thrown into the everlasting fire of hell. The foundational principles governing, directing and saving relationships in Christ and Christians are based solely on past decisions or experiences. It is not a statistic relationship, which is solely based on past decisions and experiences. It is never a statistic relationship as Christ lives in Christians and shares his divine life with his or her.

Remaining in Christ is placed upon all Christians. They must respond to God's gift of divine life and power of the Holy Spirit given at conversion the moment that Christian or non-believers give their lives to Jesus Christ as their Lord and Savior. The result is Jesus Christ continued indwelling through the power of the Holy Spirit. Christians have received fullness of joy in the Holy Spirit as well as great success in prayer. Failure to remain in Christ will lead to consequences of fruitlessness and removal from Christ that will lead to destruction of life.

Remaining in Jesus Christ calls us to a life of holy intimacy and personal devotion to him. This is going to be possible because God the Father Almighty has poured into our hearts by the Holy Spirit that indwells us, "And hope does not disappoint us, because God has poured out his love into our hearts by the Holy Spirit, whom he has given us" (Romans 5:5). All Christians experienced the love of God in their hearts through the Holy Spirit, especially in times of trouble. When the Scripture said, "God poured," it means that the Spirit of the Lord continues to flood out of hearts with love. It is this ever-present experience of God's love that keeps and sustains all the Christians in times of suffering, affliction or persecution.

God's unceasing love pouring upon Christians assures believers that hope for the future glory, that our hope for Christ's return, is assured. Christians will be thinking about something that is good that is going to happen in the future. Through confidence in God concerning his promise, which is sure, because it is based on God's integrity and of God's word, Christians will experience the reality of hope because God is the God of hope. Christian salvation lies in Christ's blood and his resurrection life; where Christ forgives our past, present and future sins, whereby believers of Jesus Christ are forgiven and reconciled to God. This experience is initial salvation.

"But now righteousness from God, apart from law, has been made known, to which the Law and the prophets testify. This righteousness from God comes through faith in Jesus Christ to all who believe" (Romans 3:21-22). This Scripture refers to humanity's sinfulness that shows and teaches that everyone is in need of the gospel of the Lord to salvation, the good news of God's grace. Forgiveness and redemptive work are in Jesus Christ only. It also proved the emphasis of the justification by grace through faith; it brought in victory over sin and the nature of sin. It also revealed life in Christ emphasizes life according to the Spirit and future Christian glorification and condition of the gospel, which shows the love of God to other in your lives. God's redemptive activity in the area of human sins by which he put all Christians in the right relationship with himself and liberated us from the power of evil where the

working of salvation and the manifestation of the righteousness of God are essentially the same thing.

"Sing to the Lord a new song, for he has done marvelous
things, his right hand and his holy arm has worked salvation
for him. The Lord has made his salvation known and revealed
his righteousness to the nations" (Psalm 98:1-2). In this prophetic psalm, the psalmist is telling all those who believe in
God to sing songs of praise to his holy name for the Lord's
victorious victory and for his redemptive work of salvation,
which was made known first to the people of Israel and then
to all the people in all the nations of earth. This prophecy was
fulfilled through the outpouring of the Holy Spirit upon all
who live in Jerusalem on the day of Pentecost and until today.

The Holy Spirit's empowerment is the proclamation of the
gospel of God; the joyful worship with the Holy Spirit's empowerment brings joyful worship that fills our hearts with
God's glory. Faith in Jesus Christ as our Lord and Savior is the
only condition that God the Father Almighty requires for salvation. Jesus calls believers to a life of holy intimacy and personal devotion to him. God demonstrated his great love for all
who believe in him, which he has poured into our hearts by the
Holy Spirit of God. God also demonstrated his great love for
humanity through Jesus Christ's atoning sacrifice dying for us
while we were still sinners. We remain in Jesus Christ because
of his love by pursuing spiritual intimacy and communion with
him and by obeying his commandments just as he did with
God the Father. Jesus Christ's life is the Christian life.

"And without faith it is impossible to please God, because anyone who comes to him must believe that he exists and that he rewards those who earnestly seek him" (Hebrews 11:6). This verse is telling us that we must believe in the existence of a personal, infinite, holy God who cares for us.

2

Christ, the Author and Finisher of our Faith

THE SCRIPTURE REVEALED, "LET US FIX OUR EYES ON Jesus, the author and perfecter of our faith, who for the joy set before him endured the cross, scorning its shame, and sat down at the right hand of the throne of God. Consider him who endured such opposition from sinful men, so that you will not grow weary and lose heart" (Hebrews 12:2-3). In all our struggles and our race for faith, Christians must look, as well as focus on, Jesus Christ our Savior Lord as our example; He came to this world from his Father's glory in heaven, placed in humanity so that he could save us from our sins. Jesus Christ trusted God the Father in everything he did while on earth. Christ always says, "For I do not speak of my own accord, but the Father who sent me commanded me what to say and how to say it. I know that his command leads to eternal life, so whatever I say is just what the Father has told me to say" (John 12:49-50). This is Jesus Christ's commitment to God the Father's will. All Christians must do the same in order to bring great glory to God. We must commit everything to Christ. We must pray without ceasing for everything we are about to do and have done. We must follow Jesus' command and do his will.

We must pray to Jesus Christ so that we can overcome temptation and suffering according to the Scripture, "Then I said, here I am—it is written about me in the Scroll. I have come to do your will, O God. First he said, sacrifices and offerings, burnt offerings and sin offerings you did not desire, nor were you pleased with them (although the law required them to be made). Then he said, here I am. I have come to do your Will. He set aside the first to establish the second, and by that will, we have been made holy through the sacrifice of the body of Jesus Christ once for all" (Hebrews 10:7-10).

Jesus Christ was obedient. He voluntarily offered himself as an atoning sacrifice for our sin. The sacrificial lamb of God is better than the involuntary animal sacrifices in the Old Testament. The once and for all offering of Jesus Christ on the cross and its benefits made salvation complete and perfect. Therefore, perfect salvation in Christ is imparted to all who have faith and come to Christ in faith. All who are made holy as they draw near to God through Jesus Christ's faith and Christians drawing near to God through Jesus Christ are inseparable. Faith is when a non-believer sincerely and truthfully comes to God through the preaching of the gospel and believing in the goodness of our Lord Jesus Christ.

By coming to God through Jesus Christ, they automatically find mercy of God, grace of God and help from God in all areas of their lives. They also find salvation, sanctification and cleansing. This indicated clearly that where there is no drawing near to God in prayers and fellowship with Jesus Christ, there is no saving faith. Jesus Christ perseveres by enduring the cross. Christians must run the test of faith with perseverance, with patience and with endurance.

The race must also be run by throwing out all sin that can easily entangle or contaminate us. By fixing our mind and our eyes on Jesus, we will be able to get victory in our walk with the Lord. We must fix our eyes on Jesus Christ in seeking the joy of the Father, in completing the work that God the Father has assigned for us. This fundamental principle is affirmed four times in the Scripture. "He who is coming will come and will not delay. But my righteousness one will live by faith. And if he shrinks back, I will not be pleased with him" (Hebrews 10:38).

Our relationship to God and our participation in the salvation is provided through Jesus Christ. The person who perseveres in faith, is strong in faith and stands firm in faith will receive what God promises and be saved. God added that if anyone shrinks back in unbelief, he will not be pleased with that person and the person will die from his own destruction, as did the Israelites in the wilderness.

Faith demonstrates that and shows Christian believers to exercise faith and trust in the Lord in all circumstances, which will enable Christians to persevere and remain steadfastly loyal to God and his word at all times in all areas of believers' lives.

"By faith he made his home in the promised land like a stranger in a foreign country; he lived in tents, as did Isaac and Jacob, who were heirs with him of the same promise" (Hebrews 11:9). Abraham rejoiced in the Lord for finding him and using him for his glory. His greatest reward is that he will be in the presence of God forever.

3

Christ, our Spiritual Life

ALL CHRISTIANS DERIVE THEIR SPIRITUAL LIFE THROUGH Jesus Christ, "But grow in the grace and knowledge of our Lord and Savior Jesus Christ. To him be glory both now and forever amen" (2nd Peter 3:18). "Submit yourselves, then, to God. Resist the devil, and he will flee from you. Come near to God and He will come near to you. Wash your hands, you sinners and purify your hearts you double—minded" (James 4:7-8). All Christians must be willing to resist the devil in everything they do; they must resist the temptation of the devil and his entire quick plan. Believers must come near God and focus on Jesus Christ for Spiritual strength at all times.

In worship, praise and thanksgiving, prayer and fasting, in fellowship with the Holy Spirit and in the word, wash your hands by confessing sin and unknown sins in your lives; get your life in the right place before God. Christians must purify their hearts by allowing God to cleanse their inner life and thoughts, our hearts, our spirit, likewise, our mind and body. These will enable believers to experience greater grace, which will result in a life of full victory over sinful nature.

To gain a spiritual life in Jesus Christ, believers must live a life of humbleness because pride will cause God to turn from our prayers and withhold his grace. God is telling us that He will give abundant grace, mercy and help in every situation of life to those who follow Christ and humbly submit to God and draw near to him.

"So that Christ may dwell in your hearts through faith. And I pray that you, being rooted and established in love, may have power, together will all the saints, to grasp how wide and long and high and deep is the love of Christ and to know this love that surpasses knowledge—that you may be filled to the measure of all the fullness of God" (Ephesians 3:17-19). Christians must have the Spirit of Christ dwell in their inner being—to have the inner being strengthened by the Spirit is to have our spirit energized with the life of Jesus Christ and to bring our soul, spirit, body, feelings, thoughts and all our purposes more and more under his control and direction so that the Holy Spirit will be able to manifest his life and power through us in a greater measure.

The purpose of the manifestation of the Holy Spirit is in three ways. This will allow Christ to establish his full presence in all Christian hearts. Christ will be able to strengthen us in our prayers "I pray that out of his glorious riches he may strengthen you with power through his Spirit in your inner being" (Ephesians 3:16). Believers are being rooted in the revelation of God's love in Christ like a tree or plant with deep roots in the soul. Being established in Christ's love is as a building with a strong foundation laid on a solid rock.

The love of Christ is necessary for a deep, solid relationship that issues forth in powerful fruit and lives to God's glory. The Scripture revealed, "You, however, are controlled not by the sinful nature but by the Spirit, if the Spirit of God lives in you.

In addition, if anyone is without the Spirit of Christ, he does not belong to Christ. However, if Christ is in you, your body is dead because of sin, yet your spirit is alive because of righteousness" (Romans 8:9-10). All Christians, from the very moment of their spiritual birth and faith in Jesus Christ, have the Holy Spirit dwell in their hearts. Without the power of indwelling of the Holy Spirit, believers will not be able to live spiritual lives that God requires from his children. The Holy Spirit must be living in your heart in order to live a Christian life.

The indwelling presence of the Holy Spirit is related to a new birth, and a new life in Christ; the Holy Spirit incorporates believers into one body of Christ. The baptism of the Holy is an empowering experience, which is related to the baptism in the Holy Spirit. It is initiation into the fullness, prophetic activity and supernatural gifts for a lifetime of witnessing in Jesus Christ's power. God's purpose is that all Christians will experience baptism in the Holy Spirit in their life. The Holy Spirit is an agent that distributes spiritual gifts to all the individual believers who are members of the church of Jesus Christ. These gifts of the Holy Spirit are a manifestation of the Spirit through all Christians by which Christ's presence, love, truth and righteousness are made real to the fellowship of believers to live a good life in Christ.

Christians cannot experience the activity of the Holy Spirit in their lives without fully separating from the world of sin and the nature of sin. Christians will experience Christ in their lives as follows: (1) the fullness of new life in Christ; (2) the righteous way of living; (3) power of witnessing for our Lord Jesus Christ, in which they will have power to witness for our Lord, or fellowship with his body; and (4) the Holy Spirit will produce righteousness through all the believers and lead them into the knowledge as well as commit them to the truth of the Bible.

Through life in the Spirit, believers will be sanctified by the Holy Spirit, which cleanses and motivates Christians to live holy lives. Christians who are delivered from the bondage of sin live a sanctified life. In a spiritual life, the Holy Spirit produces Christ-like character in us that gives glory to the ever-living Christ who never fails us and who will never fail us. Life in the Spirit helps believers to worship God in Spirit and in truth. The Holy Spirit discloses and teaches Christians to believe and continually imparts God's love in us, the supplies of our joy and comfort, guiding us into all truth, helping believers to live Christian lives.

The Scripture says, "But you will receive power when the Holy Spirit comes on you; and you will be my witnesses in Jerusalem, and in all Judea and Samaria and to the ends of the earth" (Acts 1:8). The Holy Spirit's principal work in witnessing and proclamation is based upon believers for power and their testimony to Christ's saving work and resurrection. Baptism in the Holy Spirit not only imparts power to preach about Jesus Christ as our Lord and Savior but also increases believers' effectiveness of witnessing because it strengthens and deepens the relationship with God the Father, God the Son and God the Holy Spirit, which comes when believers are filled with the Spirit.

For a spiritual life in Jesus Christ, the Holy Spirit will make the personal presence of Jesus more real to individual Christians; witness to an intimate fellowship with Jesus Christ himself will be the ever-growing desire to love him, honor him and to please him in everything that we do in his holy name. The Spirit's manifestation and empowerment is to witness with power the gospel of Jesus Christ. A believer's baptism in the Holy Spirit is the point where the Spirit-filled believers receive the enabling power of the Spirit to witness for Christ, which often comes with power to do signs and wonders and perform miracles as the Spirit gives utterance. Therefore, if the Spirit of Jesus Christ indwells and baptizes believers into the spirit who is Holy, that means the Spirit is truly at work in the life of the believer in all his fullness. They will live in greater conformity to Christ's holiness.

In the light of these Biblical truths, Christians who have been baptized in the Holy Spirit will have an earnest desire to please Jesus Christ in whatever way possible. The fullness of the Spirit complements and completes the saving and sanctifying work of the Holy Spirit in our lives. Believers must remember the experience of Pentecost, which always involves human responsibility. Believers who are in need of the Spirit's outpouring power to do God's work should make themselves available to the Holy Spirit through commitment to God's will and through prayer.

All the Christians in the world must live Spirit-filled lives in order to serve the Lord faithfully and sincerely according to his will. In a spiritual life, "No temptation has seized you except what is common to man. And God is faithful; he will not let you be tempted beyond what you can bear" (1st Corinthians 10:13). Those Christians who believe that they can securely live as Christians without turning away from unrighteous behavior and worldly passions should take good notice of the warning of God through Apostle Paul in this letter.

Apostle Paul emphasized that true Christians might not fall into sin because of temptation. The Holy Spirit explicitly affirms that God the Father Almighty provides his children with adequate grace to overcome every temptation. The Spirit of God will provide a way out so that the believer will receive God's grace, the blood of Jesus. Atoning for our sin, the word of God, and the indwelling power of the Holy Spirit together with our Lord Jesus Christ's heavenly intercession will give believers sufficient power and will help all the believers of Jesus Christ to be victorious over the power of sin and demonic influences because God's divine power has given to Christians everything they may need for life and godliness.

The Scripture also revealed, "Not only so, but we also rejoice in our sufferings, because we know that suffering produces perseverance, perseverance character; and character, hope. And hope does not disappoint us, because God has poured out his love into our hearts by the Holy Spirit whom he has given us" (Romans 5:3-5). Christians can rejoice in their sufferings because they have been redeemed for their good in Christ Jesus. All kinds of life trials may press in on us. These include those things like the pressures of financial or physical need, trying circumstances, sorrow, sickness persecution, mistreatment or loneliness. In all these troubles God's grace enables us to seek his face more diligently and produces in us a persevering spirit and proven character that will result in spiritually mature hope that will not disappoint. God's grace will help all Christian believers to look beyond their present problems to a fervent hope in God and a certain hope for the return of our Lord to establish righteousness and godliness in the new heaven and the new earth.

Right now, and in the meantime, God Almighty has poured out his love into our hearts by the Holy Spirit to comfort all the Christians who are in trials and bring them to Jesus Christ's presence. Christians have experienced the love of God; God's love is for believers in their hearts through the Holy Spirit, especially in times of troubles. All Christians are living a spiritual life through Jesus Christ our Savior who asked the Father for the comforter, Paraclate, the heavenly guest of the Holy Spirit.

"By faith Abraham, even though he was past age—and Sarah herself was barren—was enabled to become a father because he considered him faithful who had made the promise" (Hebrews 11:11). Abraham's love of God is an example to all those who believe in Jesus Christ. We are all God's people; we are all travelers, traveling through this world on our way to God's holy city, to his home that he built for us in heaven.

Christ, our Mediator of the New Covenant

"BUT THE MINISTRY JESUS HAS RECEIVED IS A SUPErior to theirs as the covenant of which he is mediator is superior to the old one, and it is founded on better promises. For this reason Christ is the Mediator of a New Covenant, that those who are called may receive the promised eternal inheritance—now that he has died as a ransom to set them free from the sins committed under the first covenant" (Hebrews 8:6, 9:15). Superior means a significant theme contrasting between the old covenant that was centered on the law of Moses and the covenant that was instituted by Jesus Christ. After Jesus looked upon him, all our past, present and future sins by giving his life as a sacrifice, he entered heaven and is seated at the right hand of God's presence on behalf of all those who believe in him.

Jesus Christ is our high priest in heaven. Christ was the priest and the sacrificial lamb of God. He sacrificed himself; he offered himself for all people in the world, as a perfect sacrifice for sin by shedding his blood and dying in the place of sinners. Jesus Christ mediates the covenant that is new and better than the old covenant in order that all who are called may receive the promise of eternal inheritance, and with confidence, they may have a continual access to God.

Jesus Christ is in heaven in God's presence to give God's grace of salvation to all those who believe, which the grace of God mediates to us through Jesus Christ, our mediator of a new covenant in heaven. Jesus Christ regenerates believers and pours out the Holy Spirit to them. Jesus Christ's activity is to mediate between God and all the humanity who have broken the law of God and they are seeking forgiveness and reconciliation for their life.

Jesus Christ, our high priest in heaven, holds the priesthood permanently and sympathetically with nonbelievers' and believers' temptations as well as helping them with all their needs. Jesus Christ lives forever in order that he will continually be in heaven for all those who have faith in him and come to God through him. Jesus will bring believers salvation into completion of his second coming to set up his kingdom on earth.

The new covenant of Jesus Christ can also be called the new covenant of the spirit, for it is through the Holy Spirit who ministers life and power to those who believe and accept God's covenant. All Christian believers who participate in the new covenant through Jesus Christ will receive blessings and salvation, as they persevere in faith and obedience. The Bible revealed that the first covenant was imperfect and incomplete. It cannot permanently take away sins of the people; it is a temporary solution until such time that God's perfect provision will manifest in his Son Jesus Christ by the redemptive work.

God Almighty has planned the new covenant before the creation of the universe. Therefore, the new covenant was always necessary and in God's plan even before the world began.

Jesus Christ is the one who initiates and the one who establishes the new covenant and his heavenly ministry is far beyond and far more superior to the ministry of Old Testament priests. The new covenant is an agreement, promise, the last will and testament and a statement of intention to be bestow divine grace and blessing on all those who believe in God; those who in sincere repentance and through faith accept Jesus Christ as the true Son of God; those who receive Jesus Christ's promise and willingly commit their lives to him personally and to the gospel of God.

"To Jesus the mediator of a new covenant and to the sprinkled blood that speaks a better word than the blood of Able" (Hebrews 12:24). With this in mind, all Christians must make every effort to live a holy life. Under the old covenant, the Israelites watched intensely for the reappearance of their high priest after he had gone into the sanctuary to make atonement. Likewise, Christians know that their high priest has entered the heavenly sanctuary as the advocate. He waits with eagerness and earnest hope for his reappearance in order to bring salvation of God by grace to its completion. The purpose of Jesus Christ, our mediator of a new covenant, is based on his sacrificial death on the cross. The promise and the obligations of the new covenant are embodied in the entire New Testament. Its main purpose is to save from guilt and condemnation all those who believe in Jesus Christ and have committed their lives to the truths and obligation of his covenant and to make them the people who are God's very own people.

The new covenant will be internalized as heart's reality, "This is the covenant I will make with the house of Israel after that time, declares the Lord. I will put my laws in their minds and write them on their hearts. I will be their God and they will be my people. "By calling this covenant new, he has made the first one obsolete; and what is obsolete and aging will soon disappear" (Hebrews 8:10, 13). God's holiness and righteousness are internalized in the believers by the Holy Spirit. God Almighty imparted a new heart and a new nature where Christians will passionately love and joyfully obey God and worship him.

The new covenant will be personal with individual Christians because God the Father said, "They will know me from the least of them to the greatest" (Hebrews 8:11). Knowing God is very personal from one individual to another. Knowing God is a community experience as well as personal experience, knowing each individual in the church and in the community of Christians as a member of the new covenant. Christ, as our high priest in heaven with his atoning blood, makes it possible for all Christians to have direct access into the most holy place of God's presence.

The new covenant will thoroughly deal with sin, the Lord said, "I will forgive their wickedness and will remember their sins no more" (Hebrews 8:12). All the new covenant Christians know quite well and fully the reality of God's forgiveness through the cleansing of individual conscience. The blood of Jesus Christ enables sin of all Christians to be blotted, canceled or erased out so that God will not remember it anymore because we are in Christ. God sees believers in Christ's righteousness.

Jesus Christ, our mediator of a new covenant in heaven at the right hand of God the Father, is mediating for us forever.

"And so from this one man, and he as good as dead, came descendants as numerous as the stars in the sky and as countless as the sand of the seashore" (*Hebrews 11:12*). God almighty blessed Abraham because of his sincere, heartfelt obedience. God speaks of a spiritual blessing that would come through Abraham's seed— God's promise to Abraham is revealed through Jesus Christ and his faithful people who proclaim the gospel to all the people on earth.

5

Christ is the same Yesterday, Today and Forever

THE SCRIPTURE SAID, "JESUS CHRIST IS THE SAME YESterday" (Hebrews 13:8). Jesus Christ will never leave us or forsake us, no matter how limited our earthly possession may be or how our circumstances and trials may be. Believers do not need to be fearful that God will leave, desert or forsake them. The Scripture tells us clearly and declares to us that the heavenly Father cares for all His children. Therefore, we can say boldly the Lord is my helper, I will not be afraid. All Christians must be affirmed with confidence in times of distress, trials and troubles. "If that is how God clothes the grass of the field, which is here today and tomorrow is thrown into the fire, will he not much more clothe you, you of little faith?" (Luke 12:28) This scripture is reassuring us that Jesus Christ was with us yesterday, taking all of our problems for us. These words of scripture contain God's promise to all His children in this troubled, unpredictable and uncertain world. God has promised to provide for our food, our clothing and all other necessities of believers. Believers need not worry if they let God reign and take total control of their lives. Jesus Christ is the same yesterday and is always the same; He never changes. The Holy One of Israel, the seed of David, will surely takes the full responsibility of those who are wholly yielded to Him. Jesus Christ is the same yesterday and today because He is the only one with the Father before the foundation of the world. Jesus Christ was the same yesterday because he completed the work of redemption that the Father assigned Him to do. Those who follow Christ are urged to seek above all else the Kingdom of God and His righteousness.

Believers must continually look many ways to get close to the Lord as well as do His will, following His commandments. Believers of Jesus Christ must make a diligent effort, absorbed, searching for something, or making strenuous ways to obtain something or do something tangible for the kingdom of God. Jesus Christ said that we must seek the kingdom earnestly to have the rule and the power of God demonstrated in our lives and in other people's lives. This is how we can experience Jesus Christ yesterday and continually experience Him today. Jesus Christ entered the Melchizedek priesthood to be our high priest in Heaven through the sacrificial atonement for our sins and the sins of the whole world. Jesus Christ was the same yesterday because He is the word incarnate. The word of God that became flesh and dwelt among us. Jesus Christ is the same yesterday and today because God, the Father, saved the world through Noah. Jesus Christ is the same yesterday and today because the blessing of the nations of the world was archived through Abraham. Jesus Christ is the same yesterday and today because the Israelites were delivered from slavery and the law was given to Moses. Jesus Christ is the same yesterday and today because the promise of the Messiah was fulfilled through David, Isaac and Jacob. Jesus Christ is the same yesterday and today because He completed the work of redemption on the cross; He went to the cross, and went through the agony and suffering on the cross in order to redeem us from our past, present and future sins. Jesus Christ is the same yesterday and today because He rose from the grave, ascended to Heaven and is seated at the right hand of God.

"Abram traveled through the land as far as the site of the great tree of Moreh at Shechem. At that time, the Canaanites were in the land" *(Genesis 12:6).* This shows that the true obedience to God is essential to a saving relationship with the Lord God. Abram obeyed the word of the Lord.

6

Christ, our Great Intercessor in Heaven

"THEREFORE HE IS ABLE TO SAVE COMPLETELY those who come to God through him, because he always lives to intercede for them" (Hebrews 7:25). Jesus Christ is at the right hand of God the Father Almighty interceding for all Christians in all the areas of their lives asking the Father for what they need on their behalf. Our Lord and Savior Jesus Christ lives in heaven in his Father's presence. He is interceding for each individual of all those who believe and every one of his followers according to the Father's will. Through Jesus Christ's ministry of intercession, believers experience God's love and presence, and they find mercy and grace to help them in times of need.

"Who will bring any charge against those whom God has chosen? Christ Jesus, who died more than that, who was raised to life, is at the right hand of God and is also interceding for us" (Romans 8:33-34). God's purpose for the human race from eternity is to love and redeem them through Jesus Christ. Intercession is a holy, believing and persevering prayer whereby our Lord and Savior is pleading with God on our behalf because of all that believers are sending to him every day through prayers of the saints and individual Christians.

Our Lord and Savior receives more than a billion prayers every second from the world. Some prayers might be emergencies, some might be immediate, some might be able to wait. He has something better than what the believer asked for. A prayer in Jesus' holy name is a prayer of intercession; it goes straight to the throne of grace where he is seated at the right hand of the Father. A prayer of intercession is received by Jesus Christ when the Christian ends it with his seal on it, which is his full name. All believers must know that they have to end their prayers with the full name of Jesus Christ. If you are praying to God and you want to receive answers to your prayers, you must learn how to end your prayer with the full name of Jesus Christ.

There is a lot of Jesus in the spiritual realm, in the space and in the air. Our Lord said, ask and you shall be given, knock and the door shall be open (Matthew 7:7). He put a clause in it; he said ask in my name. Many believers will say they have been praying but they did not receive answers to their prayers, because they fail to address their letter properly. They did not put the right stamp on it and they did not put the right name on it. Therefore, their prayer did not reach the ceiling. It does not get to the hands of our intercessor Jesus Christ our Lord. God the Father, God the son and God the Holy Spirit are forever one God. Once you address your prayer properly it gets to the hands of Jesus our great intercessor in heaven and you know that your prayers solved your problem. Your request is automatically in the hands of God the Father because Jesus Christ is seated at the right hand of God. The Scripture says, "Then Jesus came to them and said, All authority in heaven and on earth has been given to me, Therefore, go and make disciples of all nations, baptizing them in the name of the Father and of the Son and of the Holy Spirit." (Matthew 28:19).

Christians must be clear and precise in their prayers. Jesus Christ as our great intercessor in heaven. He listens to our prayers and answers our prayers because he gave us his Spirit. The Scripture revealed how the prophets and priest in the Old Testament prayed earnestly for the people of Israel. Our Lord and Savior's priestly prayer (John 17:1-26) is an intercessory prayer before he left the earth. Daniel said, "So I turned to the Lord God and pleaded with him in prayer and petition, in fasting, and in sack cloth and ashes" (Daniel 9:3). Jesus Christ is the one and only one who speaks to God the Father in our defense. He is our advocate. He is the foundation for our assurance of forgiveness and cleansing from sin, both initially and continually.

Jesus Christ intercedes before God on our behalf based on his atoning death on the cross and our active faith in him. "For there is one God and one Mediator between God and men, the man Christ Jesus, who gave himself as a ransom for all men— the testimony given in its proper time" (1st Timothy 2:5-6). Jesus Christ is our access to God and his throne of grace is exclusively through Jesus Christ as our mediator and high priest in heaven. All believers rely on Jesus Christ's sacrificial death to cover our sins and prayers of faith for strength, mercy and help in their weaknesses. Christians must not allow any other created beings to take Christ's place in their lives.

Jesus Christ is our high priestly prayer for his people as well as his desire to pour out the Holy Spirit to all believers; Christ also helps believers to understand the content of his intercessory ministry in their lives. Jesus Christ's intercession has helped those who come to God to receive the fullness of grace and salvation. Christ' intercession as our high priest is essential to our salvation; without the grace of God, mercy and help mediated to us through his intercession, we would fall away from God, once again or be enslaved to sin or condemnation because of our hope in Jesus Christ. By faith, believers are always overcomers.

Our Lord and Savior Jesus Christ's intercession does not remain an advocate and intercession for those who refuse to confess and forsake their sins, and who depart from fellowship with God. Christ will save completely only those who come to God through him. There is no safety and security for those who deliberately sin and abandon God. Since Jesus Christ is our only mediator and our only intercessor in heaven, any attempt to treat angels or dead saints as mediators and to offer prayers to the Father through them is futile and unbiblical.

The Scripture revealed, "Do not let anyone who delights in false humility and the worship of angels disqualify you for the prize, such a person goes into great detail about what he has seen, and his unspiritual mind puffs him up with idle notions"(Colossians 2:18). Some false teachers during early Christianity were saying that angels should be called on and worshiped as mediators in order for people to make contact with God. Apostle Paul made it clear to them that calling on angels would be displacing Jesus Christ as the supreme and sufficient head of the church. Consequently, Paul warns the believers against this wrong teaching by false teachers.

Today, in our society, especially in some churches, the belief that Jesus Christ is not our only mediator or intermediary between God and humans is promoted in the practice of worshiping and praying to dead saints who act as patrons and mediators. This practice robs Christ of his supremacy and centrality in God's redemptive plan. Worship and prayer to anyone other than God, the Father, God the Son, the Lord Jesus Christ and God the Holy Spirit are clearly unbiblical and must be rejected by all faithful Christians in the universe.

Christ Jesus is the one and only, our great intercessor in heaven. We must pray to him directly. We must boldly approach the throne of grace. He is there waiting for our prayers and he will answer our prayers.

"The Lord appeared to Abram and said, 'To your off-spring I will give this land.' So he built an altar there to the Lord, who had appeared to him" (Genesis 12:7). Scripture explained to us that God appeared to Abram; though it is reasonable to assume that God had already appeared to Adam and others. God's appearance could be seen as an objective, visible manifestation of God in the likeness of a human being.

7

Christ, our Redeemer King

JESUS CHRIST IS OUR REDEEMER FROM THE BEGINNING OF creation. The Scripture revealed, "My lips will shout for joy when I sing praise to you, I, whom you have redeemed" (Psalm 71:23). In another Scripture, we read, "The Lord redeems his servants no one will be condemned who takes refuge in him" (Psalm 34:22). In addition "Who redeems your life from the pit and crowns you with love and compassion" (Psalm 103:4). God forgives the human race all their sin when they come to Christ in faith; he blesses them with the gift of redemption and eternal life. Forgiveness is the first and most important gift we can receive from God. Through the forgiveness of our sins, we are restored to God and redeemed from destruction.

In another Scripture, "Let the redeemed of the Lord say, this—those he redeemed from the hand of the foe" (Psalm 107:2). In this very psalm of the Scripture, the psalmist praises and exhorts the redeemer our Lord and Savior for deliverance from desperate and dangerous situations. He made it clear that God always responds to the extreme troubles of all his people when they pray. God our redeemer King redeems us in so many ways that we cannot imagine. He frequently brings his children to a place where their own self-sufficiency fails and where no human can help them, so that they might cry out to him in humble and childlike faith.

God the Father will step in and solve that problem in as simple and miraculous a way as possible. We read in other songs of David "O Israel, put your hope in the Lord, for with the Lord is unfailing love and with him is full redemption" (Psalm 130:7). Jesus Christ is our redeemer King. He said in the Scripture, "He redeemed my soul from going down to the pit and I will live to enjoy the light" (Job 33:28). Job continues and said, "I know that my redeemer lives and that in the end he will stand upon the earth" (Job 19:25). In the midst of suffering, believers of Jesus Christ must read the Job experience in the Scripture. Job clings to his faith. He did not let his faith be shaken when he was going through diverse troubles. Job exercises great faith in God. He believes that God will deliver him in the end.

Job sees God as his redeemer, his helper. Job sees his redeemer as a relative who, with great affection, came to protect and defend and someone who can help him in times of trouble by the inspiration of the Holy Spirit. Job's testimony pointed toward Jesus Christ the redeemer who would come to save his people from sin and condemnation. "This is what the Lord says—Israel's king and redeemer the Lord Almighty; I am the first and I am the last, apart from me there is no God" (Isaiah 44:6). This is what the Lord says. God hates idols. He exposes the foolishness of making an idol or a god out of a material substance and then praying to it for help.

Even today, people make all kinds of statues and idols and bow before them in prayer and adoration, hoping that the Spirit whom the image represents will help them and deliver them. "This is what the Lord says your redeemer, the Holy

One of Israel, I am the Lord your God, who teaches you what, is best for you, who direct you in the way you should go" (Isaiah 48:17). "The redeemer will come to Zion, to those in Jacob who repent of their sins, declares the Lord." (Isaiah 59:20) The redeemer that Isaiah is referring to is Jesus Christ. He said Christ would come to those who genuinely turn from their sins and serve the Lord. God Almighty promised those who will turn from their sins and accept the Messiah that his Spirit will come upon them and his words will not depart from their mouths.

The Lord is saying that the Messiah will come and redeem everyone who believes in him from their sins. The Spirit and the word of the Lord will endorse the witness of the true church and her descendants forever. God's people must declare the gospel of God in the power and in the righteousness of the Holy Spirit. The Scripture reveals in the book of Romans, "And are justified freely by his grace through the redemption that came by Christ Jesus" (Romans 3:24). Justification by the grace of God is freely given through the redemptive work of Jesus Christ. Redemption is the work of Jesus Christ. Redemption is the means by which we produce payment for sins of humanity—the state of sin that made Christ to the world and paid ransom for our sins, with his precious blood.

Christ redeemed all of humanity from their past, present and future sins. Human beings are in need of a deliverer from their sins. Christ came and paid a ransom price for the sins of humanity with his own blood. An example of redemption in the Old Testament was the Israelites free from slavery in Egypt. "I will take you as my own people, and I will be your God. Then you will know that I am the Lord your God, who brought you out from under the yoke of the Egyptians" (Exodus 6:7). God declared the essential purpose of the covenant in Sinai; the Lord promised to redeem the Israelites from the bondage of oppression of slavery and be their God, and they will return and promise to do the will of their redeemer.

God's redemption of Israel from Egypt served as a major basis for the transfer of ownership of Israel to himself. Israel will be God's by creation and election, now and the end, now by redemptive work of Jesus Christ. "Not only so, but we ourselves, who have the first fruits of the Spirit, groan inwardly as we wait eagerly for our adoption as sons, the redemption of our bodies" (Romans 8:23). Believers possess the Holy Spirit and his blessings. They still groan inwardly, desiring their full redemption. The groaning means all Christian people of Jesus Christ are living in a sinful world that grieves them, still experiencing imperfection, pain and sorrow. The groaning expresses deep sorrow felt in all these circumstances.

They groan in travail for the birthing of God's life and the kingdom in fullness in the world and for complete redemption that will occur when Christ returns in his second coming. They groan for the glory to be revealed and for the privileges of their full rights and full benefits as children of God.

"Christ redeemed us from the curse of the law by becoming a curse for us for it is written: Cursed is everyone who is hung on a tree" (Galatian 3:13). "I have been crucified with Christ and I no longer live, but Christ lives in me, the life I live in the body, I live by faith in the Son of God, who loved me and gave himself for me" (Galatians 2:20). A Christian's relationship with Christ is a profound personal attachment to, and reliance on, our Lord. Those who have faith in Jesus Christ live their lives in intimate union with Jesus Christ, both in his death and in his resurrection.

All Christians have been crucified with Jesus on the cross. They have died to the law and received the gift of salvation and they now live through Christ for God. Because of the salvation, which is in Christ, sin no longer has control over them. All true Christians who have been crucified with Jesus Christ are now living with him in his resurrection life. Christ's strength and his love live within us. Christ became the source of all life and the center of all thoughts, words and deeds. It is through the Holy Spirit's enablement that Christ's risen life is communicated continually to all Christians.

"And do not grieve the Holy Spirit of God, with whom you were sealed for the day of redemption" (Ephesians 3:30). The Holy Spirit of God who dwells in the hearts of all believers is a person who experiences grief, pain and sorrow as Jesus himself did when he wept over Jerusalem, or before waking up Lazarus from the dead. Christians must not cause the Holy Spirit grief or pain when they ignore his presence, voice or leading. Grieving the Holy Spirit could lead to resisting the Holy Spirit. This, in turn, might lead to putting out the fire of the Holy Spirit and finally put him to shame or insult the Spirit of grace.

The Scripture revealed, "In him we have redemption through his blood, the forgiveness of sins, in accordance with the riches of God's grace" (Ephesians 1:7). Jesus Christ completed the work of redemption that the Father gave him to do on the cross. Our salvation has been completed. Jesus Christ is our ever-living redeemer. Christ, "Who is a deposit guaranteeing our inheritance until the redemption of those who are God's possession to the praise of his glory" (Ephesians 1:14). The Holy Spirit is a deposit, first installment or down payment, guaranteeing our heavenly inheritance. The Holy Spirit has been given to all those who believe and put their faith in Jesus Christ their Lord and Savior who redeemed them from their sins and made them children of God. In greater measure, believers are going to have the fullness of the Spirit and the power of God in the kingdom of God.

The reason for the increased measure of the Holy Spirit's impartation is that believers may receive more wisdom, revelations and knowledge concerning God's redemptive purposes for the present and for the future salvation of believers. All Christians may be able to experience the abundant power of the Holy Spirit in their lives. The Scripture revealed, "He did not enter by means of the blood of goats and calves; but he entered in most Holy place once for all by his own blood having obtained eternal redemption" (Hebrews 9:12). God was teaching all Christians that under the old covenant, unimpeded access to his presence was yet possible because intimate communion with him could only exist when a person's inward conscience had been cleansed perfectly.

This cleansing was possible and provided when Christ our Lord gave himself as an atoning sacrifice for our sin. Through his redemptive work, Apostle Peter said, "For you know that it was not with perishable things such as silver or gold that you were redeemed from the empty way of life handed down to you from your forefathers. But with the precious blood of Christ, a Lamb without blemish or defect" (1st Peter 1:18-19). Peter was telling believers as well as reminding them how our Lord and Savior redeemed the humanity with his precious blood on the cross; he died for the sin of you and me. Jesus Christ is our redeemer now and forever. Amen.

"In the time of Herod king of Judea there was a priest named Zechariah, who belonged to the priestly division of Abijah; his wife Elizabeth was also a descendant of Aaron" (Luke 1:5). The Gospel of Luke begins with the narratives of the ministry of John the Baptist, as well as giving us Jesus' genealogy.

8

Christ, our Savior and Lord

JESUS CHRIST IS OUR SAVIOR BEFORE THE BEGINNING OF creation. Adam and Eve fell in the Garden of Eden by committing the sin of disobedience. The Lord God Almighty said, "And I will put enmity between you and the woman, and between your offspring and hers; he will crush your head, and you will strike his heel" (Genesis 3:15). This is the first promise of God concerning the plan of redemption for the people of this universe. God Almighty predicted the ultimate victory for humanity and God over-predicted victory over Satan and evil by prophesying a spiritual conflict between the offspring of the woman, which is the Lord Jesus Christ and the offspring of the serpent, which are Satan and his followers.

God promised clearly and precisely to Adam and Eve, and this was God's first promise to the human race, that Jesus Christ would be born of a woman and would be struck beating through his crucifixion. Yet, he would rise from the dead to completely destroy and crush Satan, sin and death for the sake of salvation of the entire human race. The same is true today. There is nothing that happens in this world that God did not know and he has already known how to deal with the problem when Christ returns the second time to judge the quick and the dead and set up his new kingdom on earth. Jesus Christ is the Savior of the world.

The first promise of God the Father was fulfilled when Jesus was born of the Virgin Mary, crucified, died, buried and raised to life on the third day by God the Father and the Holy Spirit. This proved clearly without a reasonable doubt that Christ is the Savior of the world and all those who live in it. "Restore us again, O God our Savior, and put away your displeasure toward us" (Psalm 85:4), "He will call out to me, you are my Father, my God, the rock my Savior" (Psalm 89:26), "Jeshurun grew fat and kicked; filled with food, he became heavy and sleek, he abandoned the God who made him and rejected the rock his savior" (Deuteronomy 32:15).

The same is true today. The prosperity of some Christians was a major factor in their walk with the Lord just as Jeshurun did. He and all of the Israelites forget about God and enter idolatry because they are making money and all their monetary problems have been solved. They stop everything, stop praying to God and stop ministering to the sinners. History has shown repeatedly that in times of ease and prosperity, God's people are most prone to forget God and stop seeking his face. However, during times of adverse circumstances, times of need in various areas of their lives, people of God will continuously approach the throne of the grace of God earnestly and ask for helpful solutions to their various problems.

"The Lord lives. Praise be to my rock exalted be my God my Savior" Christ has always been our savior even before he came to the world in our own form. In the book of Isaiah we read, "You have forgotten God your Savior" (Isaiah 17:10). Prophet Isaiah was telling the people of his day that forgetting God is not a sin limited to the nation of Israel alone; Jesus Christ warns that the worries of this life, the deceitfulness of wealth, the pursuit of material things and the pleasure of sin can choke God's word in the life of all Christians and cause them to forget about their Lord and savior. The mighty stop praying to him daily and no longer delight in him or in his word.

When this happens, we lose God's blessing and presence. Let us look, "It will be a sign and witness to the Lord Almighty, in the land of Egypt. When they cry out to the Lord because of their oppressors he will send them a savior, and defender, and he will rescue them" (Isaiah 19:20). The Lord is saying that there will be a time that Egypt, Assyria and Israel will worship the same God together but no one knows the time and date that it will happen. Egyptian people will cry out to God. They will cry out to God because they will come to the knowledge that their affliction is coming because of God's judgment upon them. They will even erect an altar for the Lord and He will hear their cry and send them a Savior.

Many people in the world will also turn to the Lord. The Scripture revealed the word of God, "For I am the Lord, your God, the holy one of Israel, your Savior" (Isaiah 43:3a). God Almighty expresses his love for Israel and the benefits of that love. All the blessings mentioned here apply even more to those who are God's children through faith in Christ. God Almighty has created all the people in the world and he redeemed all those who belong to him through faith in Jesus Christ. All believers belong to him and he knows everyone who belongs to him by name.

When Christians pass through troubles, afflictions, tribulations and persecutions, they will not be destroyed because the Savior is always with them. All Christians are precious and honored in the sight of the Lord and Savior. They are the object of his infinite love. After the angel Gabriel gave Mary the message of the Lord, Mary said, "My soul glorified the Lord and my spirit rejoices in God my Savior" (Luke 1:47). This word of Mary expressed her own need of salvation. She was a sinner who needed a Savior and Jesus Christ is Mary's Savior. The idea that Mary herself was immaculately conceived and lived without sin is nowhere to be found in the Scripture. That teaching is the teaching of false teachers and false prophets. Mary was a sinner like you and me in need of Jesus Christ her Savior. "Today in the town of David a Savior has been born to you; he is Christ the Lord" (Luke 2:11). When Jesus Christ was born, the angel announced from heaven that this is Christ the Savior of all people in the world. Therefore, at his birth, Jesus Christ was called a savior. As a Savior, he has come to deliver all the people in the world from their sin, Satan's dominion, the ungodly world, fear, death and condemnation of believers' transgressions.

The Savior is also Christ the Lord. He has been anointed as the Messiah of God and he is the Lord who rules over his people. All those who have given their life to Jesus as their Savior must also submit to his Lordship. "And for this we labor and strive, that we have put our hope in the living God, who is Savior of all men, and especially of those who believe" (1st Timothy 4:10). Only through our Lord and Savior, we will be able to live Christian lives that God almighty requires. The book of Peter revealed, "And you will receive a rich welcome into the eternal kingdom of our Lord and Savior Jesus Christ" (2nd Peter 1:11). Christians who remain steadfast in holiness will be welcome to heaven richly with honor and rewards, whereas those who are negligent, half, and half, Christ today, other gods tomorrow, will not make it to the kingdom of God.

The book of Jude beautifully said, "To the only God our Savior be glory, majesty, power and authority, through Jesus

Christ our Lord and Savior, before all ages, now and forever more Amen" (Jude:25). All Christians must offer the fruit of our lips giving praise to his Holy name and giving thankfulness to his Holy name forever. He saved us to the utmost of our lives. He is the true Savior.

"And he will go on before the Lord, in the spirit and power of Elijah, to turn the hearts of the fathers to their children and the disobedient to the wisdom of the righteous—to make ready a people prepared for the Lord" (*Luke 1:17*). The Scriptures revealed that John the Baptist was to be like the fearless prophet Elijah; because he is filled with the Holy Spirit, John will be a preacher of moral righteousness.

9

Christel, our Great Teacher

THE SCRIPTURE REVEALED, "HE GUIDES THE HUMBLE in what is right and teaches them his ways" (Psalm 25:10). Jesus Christ is our great teacher from heaven. He will guide his people to the way of righteousness. "Does he who disciplines nations not punish? Does he who teaches man lack knowledge?" (Psalm 94:10). God Almighty disciplines and teaches all those who belong to him. He said, "But just as he who called you is holy, so be holy in all you do; for it is written, 'Be holy because I am Holy'" (1st Peter 1:15-16). Our Lord said, "A student is not above his teacher, nor a servant above his master" (Matthew 10:24). Jesus Christ was telling his disciples that they must study very hard, listened to his teaching in order to be able to spread the gospel and to continue to proclaim to the people of this world.

The good news of salvation, until he returns, Jesus was telling them not to be afraid because the Holy Spirit and the Father would sustain them. They must remain faithful to the word of God, preaching openly and truthfully as well as courageously. Our Lord said, "Therefore every teacher of the Law who has been instructed about the kingdom of heaven is like the owner of a house who brings out of his storeroom new treasures as well as old" (Matthew 13:52). The teaching of our Lord during his earthly ministry was clearly about the gospel of God. The Lord was telling believers that among his people there are some of them who are not truly in the Lord. The same is true until today; many Christians are not loyal to Christ and to his word.

"Nor are you to be called teacher, for you have one teacher, the Christ" (Matthew 23:10). We have to know that the love of believers for other believers, either brothers or Christian sisters, the love believers possess for their Christian neighbors as well as their enemies, must be superior and controlled and directed by their loving affection for and devotion to God Almighty. The first commandment is to love God, which is the best teaching in the world. Jesus Christ, during his earthly ministry, describes the character of all the religious leaders and teachers, that all that they seek was to be recognized in public places. They seek honor from the people. They are supposed to be professional religionists who appear spiritual and godly, but are quite unrighteous. They speak well, teach well of godly spiritual leaders of the past, but do not follow their practices or their commitment to God and his word and righteousness.

The Scripture continues to warn all Christians today as well, that they must be aware of false teachers and consider them as unbelievers. "A student is not above his teachers, but everyone who is fully trained will be like his teacher" (Luke 6:40). "While all the people are listen to the teaching of Jesus, Jesus said to his disciples, beware of the teachers of the Law they like to walk around in flowing robes and love to be greeted in the market places and have the most important seats in the synagogues and the places of honor at banquets" (Luke 20:45-46). Jesus Christ shows himself as a great teacher as he pointed out important things that the religious leaders and teachers were doing during that time. Believers today must be aware that within the churches there may be ministers of God's word who are of the same spirit and life as those corrupted teachers of the law in Jesus' day.

Our Lord and Savior teaches that the false teacher will appear to the people as a holy man of God, appear to be concerned about the word of God and profess love for their congregation. They might even perform miracles and signs but deep down they are false teachers; they have wrong spiritual foundations and they are not true children of God. "He came to Jesus at night and said, Rabbi, we know you are a teacher who has come from God. For no one could perform the miraculous signs you are doing if God were not with him" (John 3:2). Nicodemus, one of the Pharisees' ruling council, recognized through the teaching of our Lord and Savior that Christ is a teacher from heaven. Otherwise, he wouldn't have been able to teach the people as he thought.

On another occasion, during the teaching of Jesus Christ, "You call me teacher and Lord, and rightly so, for that is what I am. Now that I am your Lord and teacher, have washed your feet, you also should wash one another's feet. I have set you an example that you should do as I have done for you" (John 13:13-14). Jesus Christ gave all believers an example how we must have concern for one another and care for one another. This verse revealed his great teaching of how we must be one in order to be able to fulfill his great commission.

The Scripture revealed in the book of Titus, "It teaches us to say No to ungodliness and worldly passion, and to live self-controlled, upright and godly lives in this present age" (Titus 2:12). Apostle Paul stated that God's saving grace has appeared to all the people in the world. Scripture teaches that Christians must put away all the ungodly passions, pleasures and values of the present world regarding all idolatry and all abomination and lust. He commanded and empowered believers to live righteous lives while waiting earnestly for the blessed hope and appearing before our Lord and Savior Jesus Christ.

The one last point the Scripture revealed and that will clearly show you that Jesus Christ is a great teacher is as follows, "As for you, the anointing you received from him remains in you, and you do not need anyone to teach you. But as his anointing teaches you about all things and as that anointing is real, not counterfeit just as it has taught you, remain in him" (1st John 2:27). All the children of God are given the power of anointing by the Holy Spirit, to teach them and help them and lead them into all truth. Christians must remain in Jesus Christ and submit themselves to Christ and to the word of God. The Spirit helps us to understand its work of redemption, which was drawn upon the lives of all Christians. All Christian believers must study and know God's truth and learn from each other through mutual teaching of the Holy Spirit.

Believers must remain in the Son and the Father according to the Biblical revelation of the word of God. Believers must study to understand the truth or the anointing of the Holy Spirit and the important reason why they should remain in the fellowship of the body of committed Christians. Believers do not need anyone to teach them if they stay in the word of God. God the Holy Spirit will teach them and continue to teach all that they need to know about worldly lust that can contaminate the body, soul and spirit. Christians knows that Christ's teaching was transferred to the Holy Spirit when Christ went to heaven. He asked the Father for the helper, teacher, counselor and comforter of believers, the Holy Spirit. Jesus Christ said, "But the Counselor, the Holy Spirit, whom the Father will send in my name, will teach you all things and will remind you of everything I have said to you" (John 14:26). The Holy Spirit will teach all those who believe in Jesus Christ, as he taught the disciples. God the Father, God the Son and God the Holy Spirit are one God in essence and a great teacher—Christ is the greatest teacher in the world from when he came to this earth and he will continue to be the greatest teacher through eternity and during his second coming.

"In the sixth month, God sent the angel Gabriel to Nazareth, a town in Galilee, to a virgin pledged to be married to a man named Joseph, a descendant of David. The virgin's name was Mary. The angel went to her and said, "Greetings, you who are highly favored! The Lord is with you (Luke 1:26-28). The Scripture revealed to us that Mary was highly favored above all women in being chosen as the mother of Jesus Christ our Lord.

10

Christen our All in All

JESUS CHRIST WILL ALWAYS BE THE ALL IN ALL TO ALL those who believe Jesus Christ is their life, the source of their existence from this earth to eternity. The loving relationship between Christ and all his body of believers will never be broken because it was a solid rock foundation from the beginning of creation. Christ will always be the channels of blessings and the fountain from where all the goodness flows to Christians. Christ is all in all for believers because he is the beginning of the mountain when you gave your life to Jesus Christ. He sealed you with the power of indwelling of the Holy Spirit and he takes up the sole responsibility of caring for you both physically and spiritually.

The Bible said he who has the Son, has life, but he or her who does not have the Son has no life. Jesus Christ is all in all, "He is the life, the way and the truth." By the power of indwelling of the Holy Spirit, the soul is united to God and from Christ's believers have life. "I am the true vine, and my Father is the gardener" (John 15:1). Jesus describes himself as the true vine and those who believe in him as the branches. By remaining attached, glued to Christ as the source of all believers' lives, they will produce good fruit. God the Father Almighty is the gardener who takes care of the branches so that they may bear fruit. God expects all believers to bear fruit; therefore, Jesus Christ has the power in heaven and on earth to take care of all those who come to him by faith and surrender their life to him in humble adoration. Jesus Christ is all in all for all the Christians in the world because after a sinner becomes a believer in Christ and all his or her past, present and future sins are forgiven, he or she receives eternal life and the Holy Spirit's power in order to remain in Jesus Christ. With the power of the Holy Spirit, believers must accept the responsibility of salvation and continue to remain in Christ. Just as the branch has life only as long as the life of the vine flows into the branches, the same way a Christian believer has Christ's life only as long as Christ's life flows into him or her through their remaining in Christ.

Jesus Christ said, "I am the vine; you are the branches. If a man remains in me and I in him, he will bear much fruit; apart from me you can do nothing" (John 15:5). All Christians must remain in Christ. Apart from Christ, we are nothing and we cannot do anything; he is the source of our strength. Without Christ, we are nothing. Therefore, maintaining the moral code of behavior of constant, intimate communion with Jesus Christ in order to draw strength from him; obeying his commandment, remaining in his love as well as loving our neighbors, our fellow Christian brothers, and sisters, keeping our lives clean through the word, resisting all sin and yielding to the Holy Spirit's direction for our lives. Christ is all in all always and forever.

"Mary was greatly troubled at his words and wondered what kind of greeting this might be. But the angel said to her, "Do not be afraid, Mary you have found favor with God. You will be with child and give birth to a son, and you are to give him the name Jesus, He will be great and will be called the son of the Most High. The Lord God will give him the throne of his father David" (Luke 1:29-34). Mary was chosen because she found favor with God. Her humble and godly life pleased God to the point and to the extent that he chose her for his most important task.

11

Christ, our Commander-In-Chief

OUR LORD JESUS CHRIST IS THE COMMANDER-IN-CHIEF before the beginning of creation. He has always been directing, commanding and controlling his people to the righteous way, from the Old Testament to the New Testament. God always sends his messages through his messenger telling all the people of the earth the right way to live and to be godly on this earth, "But showing love to –a thousand generations of those who love me and keep my commandments" (Exodus 20:6). For the people of this world to live in peace, God sent his law through Moses, the Ten Commandment, which were written by God himself on two stone tablets and given to Moses and the Israelites. The Ten Commandments are not for the people of Israel alone. They are for everyone in the world. The Ten Commandments were provided for the Israelites to help them respond to righteous living and get close to God in gratitude for their deliverance from the bondage of slavery, and to help them to love God and love their fellow citizens.

The Ten Commandments summarize God's moral law for Israelites and describe their obligation to God and other people in the world. Jesus Christ affirmed during his earthly ministry that one jot of the word of God will not pass without been fulfilled. In the New Testament, our Lord said that the Ten Commandments are summed up by love for God and love for your neighbor. The Holy Spirit empowers all Christians to fulfill the righteous requirements of the law by loving God and others from the heart. The Ten Commandments demand believers' inner spiritual righteousness that expressed outward justice and holiness. The Scripture revealed, "Moses was there with the Lord forty days and forty nights without eating bread or drinking water. And he wrote on the tablets the words of the covenant The Ten Commandments" (Exodus 34:28). Moses was sustained without water and food for forty days and forty nights because the Lord God Almighty supernaturally sustained him during those days.

Scripture says, "But when you pray, go into your room, close the door and pray to your Father, who is unseen. Then your Father, who sees what is done in secret, will reward you. When you fast, do not look somber as the hypocrites do, for they disfigure their faces to show men they are fasting. I tell you the truth; they have received their reward in full" (Matthew 6:6, 16). The scripture is referring to the discipline of abstaining from food and water for spiritual purposes. It helps people to pray more and in the strength of the Holy Spirit. Fasting is what they called prayer without words. Fasting with prayer has several purposes to honor God the Father, God the Son and God the Holy Spirit. It helps believers to humble themselves before God in others to experience more and more of the grace of God. Most important is to experience God's intimate presence in all the areas of believers' lives.

There are three main forms of fasting presented in the Scripture: (1) a normal fast—abstaining from all food solid or liquid, but not from water and (2) the absolute fast—abstaining from both food and water, which must not pass more than three days, for the kidneys may start to shut down and the body may dehydrate. Our Lord and Savior fasted for food for forty days before he started his ministry. He gave us the command in the Sermon on the Mount. Jesus Christ gave us the beatitudes, which contain a revelation of God's principles of righteousness by which all Christians are to live through faith in the Son of God and through the power of the indwelling Spirit.

All those who belong to the kingdom of God are to have an intense hunger and thirst for the righteousness taught by Christ at the sermon on the mount, "Blessed are the poor in Spirit; blessed are those who mourn: Blessed are the meek: Blessed are those who hunger: Blessed are the merciful: Blessed are the pure in heart: Blessed are the peace-makers: Blessed are those who are persecuted" (Matthew 5:3-10). In our Lord's teaching of the beatitudes, the poor in spirit have a certain requirement for believers of Jesus Christ if they want to receive the blessings of God's kingdom; believers must be guided by God's ways and God's value, which was revealed in the Scripture and not by ways and values of the world.

Believers must be poor in spirit. They recognize that they are not spiritually self-sufficient and we are in need of the Holy Spirit life, power and sustaining grace in order to inherit the kingdom of God. Our Lord taught about those who mourn and grieve over their own weakness in relation to Almighty God's standard of righteousness and the power of his kingdom. Things that are going on in the world that grieve God are also mourned over. Christians must be sympathetic to the feelings of God and to be afflicted in our spirit over sin, immorality and cruelty that are in the world.

Those who are mourned are comforted by receiving from God the Father righteousness, peace and joy in the Holy Spirit. The Scripture revealed, "For the kingdom of God is not a matter of eating and drinking, but of righteousness, peace and joy in the Holy Spirit" (Roman 14:17). Teaching about the meek, our Lord and Savior said the meek are those who are humble and submissive before Holy God. They find their refuge in the Lord Jesus Christ and they commit their lives to him. The meek are more concerned about God's work and God's people than about themselves or about their personal problems. Therefore, the Lord Jesus Christ taught that the meek would automatically inherit the earth because he has what other people do not have, the spirit of patience and gentleness.

Our Lord teaches that when people are hunger and thirsty for righteousness it means God is working in their lives. Believers must know that this is one of the important teachings of our Lord in the Sermon on the Mount. The foundational requirement for all Christians who live a godly living is to always hunger and thirst for righteousness. All Christians' spiritual conditions throughout their lives will automatically depend on their hunger and thirst for the presence of God, the word of God, the communion of Christ, the fellowship of the Holy Spirit, the righteousness, kingdom power and the return of Jesus Christ.

Christians who do not hunger and thirst for righteousness will not be hungry for the things of God; they will not destroy all the worldly anxiety, deceitfulness of wealth, desire for things of the world and life's pleasures. They will not be able to remain in Christ. This is what happens when the hunger and thirst of believers is destroyed. They will die spiritually. For this reason, it is essential that believers will be sensitive to the presence of the Holy Spirit's convicting work in our lives. Our Lord in Matthew said, "The one who received the seed that fell among the thorns is the man who hears the word, but the worries of this life and the deceitfulness of wealth chose it, making it unfruitful (Matthew 13:22).

According to the Scripture and the teachings of our Lord, people who are made merciful by God are full of compassion and pity toward those who are suffering from either sin, the nature of sin or sorrow. The merciful will help those who are suffering by bringing or introducing them to the grace and help of God through Jesus Christ. By showing mercy to other believers God will in turn have mercy upon them.

The pure in heart are those who have been rescued, delivered from sin by God's grace and now strive without deceit to please and live a glorifying life that God would like them to live for his glory. Christians seek to imitate Christ, to have the same attitude of the heart of God, which is love for righteousness and hatred of evil. Believers will find out that only the pure of heart will see God and be the children of God, as well as dwell in his presence, both now on earth and in eternity.

In our Lord's teachings about peacemakers, our Lord said blessed are the peacemakers because they are those who have been reconciled to God. They have peace with the Lord through the cross. The scripture revealed, "Therefore, since we have been justified through faith, we have peace with God through our Lord Jesus Christ" (Romans 5:1). Peace with God is one of the important benefits that will help us to receive the blessings of God. If we have peace with God, we will be able to connect with him and all our needs will be supplied by him.

Jesus Christ teaches about persecution. All those who believe in Jesus Christ face persecution no matter where they are in the world. Persecution is an automatic inheritance for all

Christians all over the world. All those who seek to live in harmony with God's word for the sake of righteousness, those who uphold God's standards of truth, justice and purity, and who at the same time refuse to compromise with the present evil society or lifestyles of some believers and non-believers, will go through rejection, affliction, criticism and persecution and various opposition will come to them from the world but they will overcome it through the power of the Holy Spirit.

When Christians are experiencing persecution of various forms, they are to rejoice because to suffer for God imparts the highest blessings on earth. Those who suffer and endure persecution, affliction and rejection because of righteousness are promised the kingdom and heavenly rewards.

Jesus Christ is the greatest teacher the world has never known. He continues to teach us today. Our Lord said, "My command is this; love each other as I have loved you. Greater love has no one than this that he lay down his life for his friends; you are my friends if you do what I command." (John 15:12-14). Jesus Christ calls Christian believers to live a life of holy intimacy and a life of personal devotion to him. This can only be possible because of God's love for all Christians, which he has poured into every believer's heart by the Holy Spirit. All Christians are chosen out of the world and God wants them to be holy because the Lord is holy. He wants all Christians to live a life of love for one another. This is a great command from our Lord and Savior.

While in this world, Christians will be hated, persecuted, rejected and afflicted for Jesus Christ's sake. The world and things of the world are the great opposition of Christ and people who belong to Christ from the beginning of creation, including all the false religious organizations and churches. They will always oppose God and the principles of his kingdom;

therefore, the world will always remain an enemy and the persecutor of faithful believers until Christ returns. The last commandment of the commander-in-chief, our Lord Jesus Christ, affirms the fulfillment of the law, "Do not think that I have come to abolish the Law or the prophets; I have not come to abolish them but to fulfill them. I tell you the truth, until heaven and earth disappear, not the smallest letter, not the least stroke of a pen, will by any means disappear from the Law until everything is accomplished" (Matthew 5:17-18). Jesus Christ did not come to the world to abolish the Old Testament revelation but rather to see that it was fulfilled in the lives of those who believe in him.

Christians are responsible to keep all the moral principles of the Old Testament as well as all the teachings of Christ and the apostles. The law reveals God's moral nature and his will for the lives of his children and, therefore, continues today. The Old Testament laws, which applied directly to the Israelites sacrificial ceremonial, social or civil laws are no longer binding. All Christians must not view the law as a system of legal commandments by which they need to obtain merit for forgiveness and salvation, but the law must be seen as a moral code for all those who are already in a saved relationship fellowship with the Lord and obey the law expressing it through the life of Jesus Christ within themselves.

Faith in Jesus Christ is the point of departure for the fulfillment of the law. Through faith in Christ, God becomes our Father. Therefore, our obedience as believers is done not only out of our relationship of children to their Father. Through faith in Christ, all the believers have received the power of the grace of God, the power of the indwelling of the Holy Spirit, and the power to fulfill God's law because with the power of the indwelling spirit of God, believers were able to live according to the spirit of God. The Holy Spirit helps all the believers to put to death the misdeeds of the body and to fulfill God's will for their lives.

The last commandment of our commander-in-chief is the great commission, "Therefore go and make disciples of all nations, baptizing them in the name of the Father, and of the Son, and of the Holy Spirit and teaching them to obey everything I have commanded you And surely I am with you always, to the very end of the age" (Matthew 18:19-20). Our great commander-in-chief Jesus Christ said these words before his ascension to all who follow him from now to eternity. The church is to go to all the nations of the earth. The church is to go into all the world. Their goal is to commission the missionary. It is a great task to preach, teach and witness the gospel to all the people in the world.

The primary responsibility of all the churches is to send missionaries into every nation. Preaching of the gospel must be centered on repentance and forgiveness of sins. The purpose is to makes disciples, not just converts, who will abide in Christ and follow and observe Christ's commands. The main objective is to make disciples who separate themselves from the world, observe the commands of Christ and follow Christ with all their hearts, minds, wills and bodies. Jesus Christ, the one and only commander-in-chief, commands us to concentrate on placing the lost men and women into his holy hands. He commanded that those who believe in him must be baptized. They are to be baptized with water. They must believe and understand the gospel of God and study the word of God in the Bible.

The water baptism represents their covenant pledge that shows that they have renounced all the immorality of the world and their own sinful nature and unreservedly committed themselves to Christ and his kingdom purpose. Christ promised that he would be with those who obediently follow in the presence and power of the Holy Spirit. They are to go to all nations only after they have been clothed with power from on high. Jesus promised that his presence and authority would be with all the believers. Jesus Christ is presently with us through the power of the Holy Spirit.

Our Lord and Savior Jesus Christ commanded the Devil during the Devil's temptation against him, "Jesus answered it is written: do not put the Lord your God to the test" (Luke 4:12). Immediately, the Devil finished all his temping. He left him alone. On another occasion, "Jesus turned and said to Peter, get behind me, Satan, you are a stumbling block to me, you do not have in mind the things of God, but the things of men" (Matthew 16:23). Our Lord commanded Satan to stay away from Peter, who needed to be more for the things of God rather than worldly material things. Jesus came to this earth to destroy the work of Satan and deliver people of the world from the dominion of Satan and to establish the kingdom of God.

Our Lord was walking beside the Sea of Galilee. He saw two brothers, Peter and Andrew, James' son of Zebedee and his brother John. With one word of command he said, "Come, follow me, and I will make you fishers of men. At once they left their nets and followed him" (Matthew 4:18-20). The disciples did and they became the fishers of men. They took the gospel to the ends of the world. Jesus Christ's command is always short and precise. He always gets to the point. Christ commanded Satan to get behind him and he did. The Devil and Satan immediately left him and went away because they know that Christ is the King of kings and the Lord of lords.

They also recognize his sovereignty over all in heaven and in the universe.

All Christians are to follow the commands of the commander-in-chief. Christ commands the people of this world to repent, "From that time on Jesus begin to preach repent for the kingdom of heaven is near" (Luke 13:3). Jesus said, "Peace be with you. As the Father has sent me, I am sending you" (John 20:21). Jesus commanded the disciples and sent them to the world just as the Father sent him to the world. Jesus Christ continuously carried out the role of a commander-in-chief. He replied to the man, "You may go, your son will live" (John 4:50). We must believe in Jesus' word with faith. Before the man got home his son was completely healed.

The commander-in-chief said that all his followers should love God as the first and important greatest commandment of the law of God, "Love the Lord your God with all your heart and with all your soul and with your entire mind. This is the first and greatest commandment" (Matthew 22:37-38). People of this world must know there is God and God asks all those who believe in Christ and receive his salvation to have a devoted love. This love involves the affection of our hearts whereby God is to be valued and esteemed. We long for his friendship, love him with all our hearts of obedience and seek his honor and glory on earth. If we truly love God the Father almighty, we will have no shame about our public identification with him even to the point of suffering for his name and righteousness. Our love of Jesus Christ must be wholehearted, must be a dominating love, a love that is inspired by God's love for us whereby he gave his Son for us.

Jesus Christ commanded us to love our neighbor. He said, "And the second is like it; love your neighbor as yourself. All the law and the prophets hang on these two commandments"

(Matthew 22:39-40). Our Lord and Savior Jesus Christ commanded Christians that they are the children of God and they are required to love all the people in the world. God wants us to pray for our enemies; Christians are also commanded to love all the true born again Christians in a special way. The love of all Christians for fellow believers, brothers and sister, neighbors and enemies must be subordinated to, and controlled and directed by their loving affection for, and devotion to, God.

Christians must put the love of God first, which is the greatest commandment; with this in mind, Christians must not compromise in their daily practice of their love for all people. Yet, it must not overpower the supremacy of their love for God and the righteous stand of the word of God. Jesus Christ commanded all believers to watch and pray, "Therefore, keep watch because you do not know what day your Lord will come. Watch and pray so that you will not fall into temptation. The spirit is willing, but the body is weak" (Matthew 24:42, 26:41). Christians should be on their knees every day, as we do not know when our Lord will return.

Jesus Christ, warning that his disciples must always be ready, was understood as referring to his return from heaven to take his saints to heaven. Jesus Christ commanded and stated that His second coming would be unexpected, anytime and without any announcement. Christians must pray at all times for the coming of the Lord. There will be no warning signs and Christians must know he can come any moment. Let them pray without ceasing to the Lord giving thanks to his return.

Our Lord commanded that if we love him we must keep his command, "If you love me, you, will obey what I command" (John 14:15). All Christians must be able to follow our Lord's commandment, in order to follow him and love him.

To show our love for him, we prove our love for him by doing what he commands us to do and not to do. Christians must be devoted to do God's will. Jesus Christ also commanded believers to ask him what they needed, "You may ask me for anything in my name; and I will do it" (John 14:4). Jesus Christ commanded that we should ask in his name. This involves at least two things; believers should pray according to Christ's will and character and they must believe that he listens to their prayers and he will fulfill their requests.

Believers are praying with faith in Christ and in his authority, and with the desire to glorify the Father and the Son. Praying in the name of Jesus, therefore, means that Christ will answer any prayer that he himself would have prayed to the Father. All Christians should know that there is no limit to the power of prayer when addressed to Jesus or to the Father in holy faith according to God's desire. The Scripture revealed in Paul's letter, "Endure hardship with us like a good soldier of Christ Jesus. No one serving as a soldier gets involved in civilian affairs—he wants to please his commanding officer" (2nd Timothy 2:3-4).

All Christians, pastors, ministers and reverends of the gospel who remain loyal to the Lord Jesus Christ and the gospel of God will be called on to endure hardship like soldiers. They must be willing through difficulties and suffering to wage spiritual warfare in wholehearted devotion to the Lord. They must be able to endure hardship in any circumstances and continue to serve the Lord. There is no retirement in the service of the Lord. It must be done until Christ calls them home for another assignment in heaven.

"And he will reign over the house of Jacob forever; his kingdom will never end. How will this be, Mary asked the angel, since I am a virgin? The angel answered, The Holy Spirit will come upon you and the power of the Most High will over-shadow you. So the holy one to be born will be called the Son of God" (Luke 1:33-35). Our Lord Jesus Christ was conceived of the Holy Spirit and was born of a virgin.

12

Christ, our Hope of Glory

T HE SCRIPTURE REVEALED, "ON THE DAY HE COMES TO be glorified in his holy people and to be marveled at among all those who have believed" (2nd Thessalonians 1:12). We pray this so that the name of our Lord Jesus may be glorified in you and you in him, according to the grace of our God and the Lord Jesus Christ. The Scripture revealed that from the beginning of creation the main issue in humanity's relationship with God has been to disregard the word of truth of the word of God or to love them. This is a pivotal issue in these last days of the end of the age. Glorious salvation will be experienced by those who through faith in Christ fervently and sincerely love the truth. "Sing to the Lord, for he has done glorious things; let this be known to the entire world" (Isaiah 12:5). Jesus is our hope of glory; God's people will praise him when the universal reign of the Messiah begins. Even now, all believers must pray for and anticipate in faith and hope of our Lord's return and the establishment of his eternal reign in righteousness. When that day comes, we will sing this song of praise. "In that day he Lord Almighty will be a glorious Crown, a beautiful wreath for the remnant of his people (Isaiah 28:5). Prophet Isaiah prophesied about Israelites denouncing their sins and apostasy and he revealed the coming judgment of God.

The judgment will be to purify God's chosen people and to bring the remnant of all the Israelites who are holy. Our Lord Jesus Christ is our hope of glory full of love and righteousness. "It always protects, always trust, always hopes, and always perseveres" (1st Corinthians 13:7). Apostle Paul described the activity of love that Jesus Christ has for those who love him and do his will. He said love as an activity and a behavior, not just an inner feeling or motivation. The various aspects of love included here characterize God the Father, Son and the Holy Spirit.

All Christians must seek to grow in the love of Jesus Christ as part of our hope of glory. Jesus Christ is our hope of glory prayed for all believers in his priestly prayer, "My prayer is not that you take them out of the world but that you protect them from the evil one" (John 17:15). The Lord Jesus Christ prayed for all the believers before he went to the cross. The evening before his crucifixion Jesus Christ prayed that his disciples and all who would believe in him after them would be holy people, separated from the sin and the world for the purpose of worshiping and serving the Lord. Believers must be set apart for the glory of their Lord and God, in order to get close to God and to live for his glory forever.

This sanctification will be accomplished by Christian devotion to the truth revealed to them by the Holy Spirit, the spirit of truth, which is the living word of God. Jesus Christ separated himself in order to do the will of the Father. All Christians should follow in Christ's footsteps and separate from the world in order to do the will of God for all their lives.

"Even Elizabeth your relative is going to have a child in her old age, and she who was said to be barren is in her sixth month. For nothing is impossible with God" (Luke 1:36-37). The angel said, nothing is impossible with God because He is the omniscience all knowing. God knows everything on earth because he is the creator. God is the omnipotent. He is all-powerful. The nature of God is infinite. He has power, mighty power. God is omnipresent. God has the ability to be everywhere at all times. God reveals Himself in His word as being everywhere.

13

Christ Jesus, our Sin Bearer

THE SCRIPTURE REVEALED THAT JESUS CHRIST CAME to this world to take away our sins. The Scripture says, "The next day John saw Jesus coming toward him and said, look, the Lamb of God, who takes away the sin of the world" (John 1:29). Jesus is the Lamb of God provided by God to be sacrificed in the place of sinners. That is why Jesus is called the sin bearer by all Christians in the world.

In Jesus Christ's death on the cross, he provided for the removal of guilt. The power of sin was destroyed and he opened the way to God for all the people of the world. "They are to take some of the blood and put it on the sides and tops of the door frames of the houses where they eat the Lambs" (Exodus 12:7). The Passover lamb and its blood pointed to Jesus Christ and his atoning sacrifice of shed blood as the Lamb of God who takes away the sins of the whole world.

The Scripture revealed in Isaiah, "He was oppressed and afflicted, yet he did not open his mouth; he was led like a lamb to the slaughter and as sheep before her shearers is silent, so he did not open his mouth" (Isaiah 53:7). Jesus Christ endured his suffering for us patiently and voluntarily. Christ is the true sin bearer of believers. Jesus Christ is coming back; he will judge the nations on his second coming. He will judge all those who oppose God's kingdom and his righteousness.

Jesus Christ is our sin bearer from the beginning of creation, "Surely he took up our infirmities and carried our sorrows, yet we considered him stricken by God, smitten by him, and afflicted, but he was pierced for our transgressions, he was crushed for our iniquities the punishment that brought us peace was upon him, and by his wounds we are healed and the Lord has laid on him the iniquity of us all He was oppressed and afflicted, yet he did not open his mouth; he was lead like a lamb to the slaughter; so he did not open his mouth. Yet it was the Lord's will to crush him and cause him to suffer" (Isaiah 53:4-6b, 7a, 10a).

Jesus Christ our sin bearer, the Messiah, endured punishment so that sinners may be delivered from their sins, diseases and sicknesses. Jesus Christ bore our sins. He took upon him the iniquities, the infirmities of human kind. He carried all our sins so that we could be free. Christ was crucified because of the sins of the human race. Christ, as our sin bearer, took the punishment due us and he paid for the penalty of our sins and the penalty of death. Therefore, we can receive the forgiveness of our sins to holy God and have peace with God. We were healed by his wounds; we have been clean by the blood of the lamb. We received the gift of salvation with all the benefits, both physical and spiritual.

Jesus Christ, our sin bearer, goes through great pain, suffering, disappointment, sorrows and grief because of our sins. Likewise, all Christians will experience a measure of suffering and rejection. Christ was despised, rejected and hated by Israel's ruling council Pharisee, Sadducees and Sanhedrin. As our sin bearer, Christ was led to the altar voluntarily. God's redemptive purpose of bringing people of this world to salvation has been accomplished through his Son. The Messiah accomplished the purpose of God; salvation is complete and perfected forever through our Lord Jesus Christ. "For he bore the sin of many, and made intercession for the transgressors" (Isaiah 53:12b). The great inheritance of Jesus Christ's death on the cross has been released to God's people.

Any church or church denomination that does not proclaim the gospel of God by preaching the cross of Christ and its deliverance from the power of sin is automatically going to fail because the cross is where all our past, present and future sins were forgiven. On the cross, Jesus Christ poured out his life onto death for the sin of all the people in the world. He is our sin bearer forever. Those who believe in him, in his word and in his atoning sacrifice and surrender their life to him will receive a new life, the gift of salvation and the gift of grace; they will also live with him in heaven.

The Scripture revealed to us, "I have swept away your offenses like a cloud, your sins like the morning mist return to me, for I have redeemed you" (Isaiah 44:22). Jesus Christ, our sin bearer, has washed away our sins and redeemed us from our sins. At the last super, "While they were eating, Jesus took bread, gave thanks and broke it, and gave it to his disciples, saying, take and eat; this is my body. Then he took the cup, gave thanks and offered it to them, saying, drink from it, all of you. This is my blood of the covenant, which is poured out for many for the forgiveness of sins" (Matthew 26:26-28). Forgiveness of sins is very important in the lives of human beings. Forgiveness is necessary because we have all sinned and are in need of a deliverer, because sin has caused us to be alienated relationally from God and we are subject to condemnation and the wrath of God. Forgiveness was possible through our sin bearer Jesus Christ's death on the cross. Therefore, our sin bearer made our relationship with God possible.

We have the Scripture word of God in the book of Hebrews, "Unlike the other high priests, he does not need to offer sacrifices day after day, first for his own sins, and then for the sins of the people. He sacrificed for their sins once for all when he offered himself" (Hebrews 7:27). "So Christ was sacrificed once to take away the sins of many people; and he will appear a second time, not to bear sins, but to bring salvation to those who are waiting for him" (Hebrews 9:28).

The blood of Jesus Christ is the central concept of redemption on the cross. Jesus Christ shed his innocent blood in order to remove our sins and reconcile us to God. By Christ's precious blood he accomplished many things: (1) His blood forgives the sins of all those who repent their sin and believe in his atoning sacrifice; (2) His blood ransoms all believers from the power of Satan and from all the evil powers; (3) His blood justifies all who believe in him; (4) His blood cleanses the consciences of all Christians that they might serve God without guilt in full assurance of faith; (5) the blood of Jesus Christ sanctifies God's people; (6) His blood opens the way to all Christians to come directly before the throne of God through him in order to find grace, mercy, help and salvation; (7) Jesus Christ's blood is a guarantee of all the promises of the new covenant; and (8) the blood of Jesus Christ has saving, reconciling, and purifying power, which continually is appropriated to Christians of all ages as they come to God through him.

Under the Old Testament and the old covenant, the Israelites watched and waited intensely for the reappearance of their high priest after he entered the sanctuary to make atonement. The same thing is happening today. Christians, knowing that our high priest has entered the heavenly sanctuary as our advocate, wait with eagerness and hope for the Lord Jesus Christ to reappear to bring salvation to its completion. Jesus Christ is our sin bearer now and forever. Amen.

"Blessed is she who has believed that what the Lord has said to her will be accomplished! And Mary said, 'My soul glorified the Lord and my spirit rejoices in God my Savior, for he has been mindful of the humble state of his servant. From now on all generations will call me blessed'" (Luke 1:45-48). Mary was favored by God because she submitted herself completely to God's will and she trusted in God's message.

14

Christ, the Life Changer

J ESUS CHRIST IS THE CHRISTIANS' LIFE CHANGER BECAUSE according to the Scripture revelation, "You diligently study the Scriptures because you think that by them you possess eternal life. These are the Scripture that testify about me, yet you refuse to come to me to have life" (John 5:39). Jesus Christ called everyone to come to him. He is the only one who changes life. In another Scripture, Jesus said, "I am the vine, you are the braches" (John 15:5). After we have been changed, we must remain in Christ; Christ is the life of all Christians. Scripture revealed " Therefore, rid yourselves of all malice and all deceit, hypocrisy, enmity, and slander of every kind like a new born babies, craves pure spiritual milk, so that by it you may grow up in your salvation, now that you have tasted that the Lord is good" (1ˢᵗ Peter 2:1-3). Christians must maintain the moral absolutes of God's word, which will stand long after today's relativism has collapsed in self-destruction.

All Christians, old or new convert believers, should produce the pure nourishment of God's word, which is a sure sign of spiritual maturity of good health. It is also a deep desire to feed on the living and enduring word of God. After Christians have been changed, they should be at alert lest their spiritual hunger and thirst for God and his word diminish or are destroyed entirely by wrong behavior. A changed believer is to intercede and pray for one another and for all people because they now processed a new life and a changed life in Christ. After a Christian has been changed, he or she will declare the word and pray for the success of God's word.

The Scripture revealed, "God opposes the proud but gives grace to the humble. Humble yourselves, therefore under God's mighty hand, that he may lift you up in due time. Cast all your anxiety on him because he cares for you" (1st Peter 2:1-2, 5b, 7). Humility should be the main character of all God's people.

Christians must not be proud; they must possess an honest awareness of their own weaknesses and the disposition of their old life in order to ascribe to God's way of life as taught in the Scriptures. Christians should put Christ on every day so that they do not fall into sin or the nature of sin. Jesus Christ is the only one who changes life. The Scripture revealed, "In a flash, in the twinkling of an eye, at the last trumpet. For the trumpet will sound, the dead will be raised imperishable, and we will be change. For the perishable must clothe itself with the imperishable and the mortal with immortality. When the perishable has been clothed with the imperishable and the mortal with immortality, then the saying that is written will come true: Death has been swallowed up in victory" (1st Corinthians 15:52-54).

Jesus Christ is the one who changes life because he is the resurrection and the life. The resurrection of the body is very essential. It refers to God's power after he raised Christ from the dead. He will raise all the human body that belongs to Christ from the dead and reunite it with the believers' spirit and soul, which was separated at death.

The resurrection of the body is necessary for all Christians in order for them to live eternally with Christ in heaven. Human beings will not be complete without the body. Therefore, the resurrection of the body is necessary. The redemptive work of Jesus Christ, the offer applies to the entire human personality, the entire person including the body. The resurrection of the body is essential. This is where believers in the whole world will see clearly and precisely what God the Father, God the Son and God the Holy Spirit have done for humankind.

The body is the temple of the Holy Spirit who dwells in all Christians. Therefore, the body will also be the temple of the Holy Spirit at the resurrection. The final enemy, the death of the body, will be permanently conquered through the resurrection of the body. There is no death in the life of believers of Jesus Christ. It is just a change of one place to another because the lives of believers in Christ flow together with Christ's life. Christ lives and believers live with him. A body changed into a heavenly body that will be automatically adapted for and prepared for the new heaven and new earth.

Believers' bodily resurrection has been and is guaranteed because our Lord and Savior was resurrected from the dead, and he said clearly, "I am the resurrection and the life" (John 11:25). A resurrection body that Christ will give all believers specifically is a body that possesses the continuity as well as the identity with the body of this present life and it will be recognizable, touchable and never decay. It is an imperishable body, free from decay and death—it is a glorifying body, like Christ's body, a powerful clean body that is not subjected to disease or weakness. It is a spiritual body, not a natural but very supernatural body, not bound by the law of nature such as hurricanes, or storms, heat waves or volcanos. Moreover, it is a body that is capable of eating or drinking as our Lord eats with disciples after his resurrection at the Sea of Galilee and with the disciple men and women on the road to Emmaus.

Christ changes life because when Christians receive their resurrection body, they will put on immortality; believers will be what the God Almighty wanted them to be at the beginning of creation. Believers will come to know God in full as he intended them to know him, and they will be able to worship him in spirit and in truth. God will be able to express his love to his children as he desires. The saints who are still alive at the time of Christ's return will experience the same bodily transformation just as those who have died in Christ many years before them. They will be given a new body as they gave to those who are raised from the dead. They will never experience physical death. Only in Christ is a new life and in him only is life changed.

"For the Mighty One has done great things for me—holy is his name. His mercy extends to those who fear him, from generation to generation" (Luke 1:49-50). Mary willingly accepted the honor and the reproach that being the mother of the holy child would bring. Our young women in the church should follow Mary's example in sexual purity, love for God, faith in his word and a willingness to obey the Holy Spirit.

15

A New Life in Christ

THE VERY MOMENT A SINNER REPENTS AND ASKS JESUS Christ to forgive him or her, the sinner's new life begins. The Scripture revealed, "Therefore, if anyone is in Christ, he is a new creation; the old has gone, the new has come. All this is from God, who reconciled us to himself through Christ and gave us the ministry of reconciliation: That God was reconciling the world to himself in Christ, not counting men's sins against them and he has committed to us the message of reconciliation" (2nd Corinthians 5:17-19). God, in his creative order, commanded that those who repent their sin and accept Jesus Christ by faith are made a new creation that totally and fully belongs to God and they will be qualified for a new earth, which will be ruled by the Spirit of God.

The believer will begin a new life, a new person renewed after God's image, sharing his glory, with new knowledge of God, with wisdom of God and understanding, living a holy acceptable life in the sight of God. The ministry of reconciliation is one of the essential aspects of Jesus Christ's work of redemption and restoration of sinners to a state of fellowship with God the Father, Son and Holy Spirit. Reconciliation was made possible and became very effective for all Christians through Christian repentance from sin and strong faith in Jesus Christ.

Church preaching, teaching and witnessing proclamation of the gospel of God is the ministry of reconciliation of Christ. Calling all people to know God, repent from sin and live a life of love of God and love your neighbor. "The fear of the Lord is the beginning of wisdom; all who follow his precepts have good understanding to him belongs eternal praise" (Psalm 111:10). When we have new life in Christ, we must continuously praise the Lord for his physical and spiritual blessings in our lives. We must thank him for his providential care over all Christians who love the Lord and fear him. When Christians love the Lord they will fear him. They will not want to offend him. They will follow his command and pray to him so that they can be able to do his will for their lives through the power of the Holy Spirit.

It is good to praise and honor God spontaneously every day of our lives. The truth of the fear of the Lord, which is the beginning of wisdom, will serve as a foundation for the spiritual growth of believers. God fearing Christians do the best thing in life and they always strive that God's will be done in their lives. With a new life in Christ we can say as the psalmist says, "The Lord is with me; I will not be afraid what can man do to me" (Psalm 118:6). The Lord will always be with his people. Those who take refuge in the Lord are guaranteed and assured that the Lord is with them to help them. Strengthening them at all times, he will never be moved. A new life in Christ the Christian believers will say, "Oh, how I love your Law I meditate on it all day long" (Psalm 119:97).

With our new life in Christ, sometime Jesus will allow us to experience hardships and troubles in order to draw us into his word and especially to himself and he can be able to help us and care for us as Father cares for his children. It also allows God to show us his love and affection. Christian life in Christ must not be afraid, "Do not be afraid of those who kill the body but cannot kill the soul, rather, be afraid of the one who can destroy both soul and body in hell" (Matthew 10:28). All the servants of the Lord and all those who believe in him should not be afraid or fear death because leaving this earth does not end but continues either in the presence of God or in a place of torment and punishment. Our Lord and Savior teaches that there is a place of eternal punishment for those who are condemned before God.

The reality and main importance is that there is a place of punishment for those who do not believe in God as well as the separation of nonbelievers from the people of God. God the Father sent his Son to die for us on the cross in order that no one perish. Our Lord said, "If anyone would come after me, he must deny himself and take up his cross daily and follow me" (Luke 9:23). A new life in Christ means accepting Jesus as Lord and Savior. This demands not only believing the truth of the gospel, but also committing one's own life to follow him sacrificially. Believers must deny themselves, put away all their selfish ambitions and desires, to follow Christ daily, and do his will. A New life in Christ, Christians must live in fellowship with their ever-living Lord, basing their total lives on the teaching of his word and find true life and joy, now and forever.

In another Scripture, our Lord said, "All that the Father gives me will come to me, and whoever comes to me I will never drive away" (John 6:37). Our Lord and Savior promises to welcome all who come to him by faith and in repentance and they come to him with the grace of God that was given to them. Scripture revealed, "Do you not know that your body is a temple of the Holy Spirit who is in you, whom you have received. From God, You were bought at a price. Therefore, honor God with your body" (1st Corinthians 6:19-20). All Christians has been blessed with the Holy Spirit. Their body is the personal dwelling place of the Holy Spirit where the Spirit put God's mark on you that you belong to him. The Holy Spirit lives inside all believers as long as they totally belong to God in total obedience and surrender. The Christian body must never be defiled by any impurity or evil, whether by immoral thoughts, desires, deeds, films, books or magazines. Christians must live in a way to honor and please God with their body, which is the temple of the Holy Spirit.

We read in the Scripture, "Finally, a brother, pray for us that the message of the Lord may spread rapidly and be honored just as it is with you" (2nd Thessalonians 3:1). A new life in Christ calls for all Christians to pray for all believers, all the body of Christ in heaven and on earth. Apostle Paul was telling us that he was able to accomplish what he did through the prayers of the saints. Therefore, it should be the same today that all believers must pray for each other. We all need prayer intercession in the church from individual believers, so that God's desires will be accomplished. Satan's purposes will be destroyed in the lives of God's people and the Holy Spirit. Power will be manifest in all the areas of Christian lives.

Sins must be confessed and fervent prayer for one another in the body of Christ must be increased and unceasing prayer be made to God. Unconfessed sin in the church hinders prayers of believers and can even block God's power of healing diseases in the congregation. The prayers of all the righteous people bring them near to the throne of Grace where the blessings of the Lord were pouring down to those who call on him.

"He has performed mighty deeds with his arm; he has scattered those who are proud in their inmost thoughts. He has brought down rulers from their thrones but has lifted up the humble" (Luke 1:51-52). You can see that Mary recognizes her own needs of salvation. She knows that she was a sinner who needed Christ as her Savior. The idea that Mary herself was immaculately conceived and lived without sin is nowhere taught in the Scripture.

16

Christ Jesus, Baptizer of the Holy Spirit

THE SCRIPTURE REVEALED, "JESUS CAME FROM GALILEE to the Jordan to be baptized by John, I need to be baptized by you, and do you come to me. As soon as Jesus was baptized, he went up out of the water. At that moment heavens was opened and he saw the Spirit of God descending like a dove and lighting on him. And a voice from heaven said; this is my Son, whom I love; with him I am well pleased" (Matthew 13:13-14, 16-17). Jesus Christ was baptized by John the Baptist before Christ's baptism. John told the crow he only baptized for repentance, which is accompanied by the fruit of righteousness with true saving faith; they must forsake sin and bear godly fruit. John teaches that the work of the coming Messiah will involve baptizing all Christians with the Holy Spirit, which is a baptism that will give a believer great power to live a life of witnessing, preaching, teaching and doing everything for the glory of God in the power of the Holy Spirit. Therefore, John's baptism for repentance is preparing the people of God for the baptism of the Holy Spirit.

Jesus Christ was baptized by John, but God the Father baptized Jesus Christ with the Holy Spirit when the dove was descending upon him. Jesus Christ was baptized by John in order to fulfill the righteous requirement of the will of God. You will see that the heavens open when he came out of the water and the Holy Spirit descended to empower him for the work of the ministry that he came to do. As the Scripture revealed in the Old Testament, God's kingdom comes not by any human might or power but by God's Spirit and his anointing. Jesus Christ came to identify himself with the sinners. This is the meaning of incarnation; Christ came to this world to identify with sinners, those he came to save by his atoning death on the cross.

This must be clear to all people; Jesus was not baptized by John for repentance. Christ is sinless, but he was baptized to identify himself with the sinners that he came to save. The Spirit descended immediately because it was time for him to begin his ministry work that he came to do. Jesus did every-thing that he did on earth with the Spirit power without meas-ure, His teaching and preaching, his healings, his suffering and his victory over sin. Jesus Christ was not alone; he did his work by the power of the Holy Spirit. The same should be for all Christians today. We should seek the power of the Holy Spirit in everything we are doing, or we are about to do, for the Lord. We must do it with the Spirit power not on our own power. Our Lord Jesus Christ said, "The Father that is in me do all the work, I do everything according to my Father's direction I am not alone." Christians today must not work alone; we must do everything for the Lord with the Spirit power.

Christians needs the Spirit power of enablement to help us to serve the Lord. We need the Spirit equipment to pray, teach, preach and witness about the Kingdom of God to non-believ-ers in the power of the Holy Spirit. Jesus Christ will baptize his people, those who follow him by faith with the Holy Spirit. He will not let them do the work alone. Jesus will baptize with the

Holy Spirit so that they might have the Spirit's enablement directing, controlling, guiding and helping working in the lives of believers to change the entire people of the world from evil to good, from the power of Satan into the power of God. Change them from non-believers to believers of Jesus Christ.

The baptism of Jesus Christ is a striking manifestation of the fact of the Trinity. During his baptism in the river Jordan, the presence of the trinity was revealed. Christ came out of the water. The Spirit descended like a dove upon him. The Father spoke from heaven and gave the affirmation, declaring and acknowledging that Christ is God's beloved Son. In him, God the Father was well pleased. Therefore, we have three equal divine persons, the Holy Trinity—Trinitarian understanding of God teaches us that these three divine persons exist before the beginning of creation in such unity that they are one God. All three persons of the Trinity are involved in Jesus Christ's baptism; they are one in essence, existing in three distinct persons who also share a common divine nature.

In other words, the Scripture revealed that God is one—a perfect unity of one nature and essence of the persons in the Godhead. None is God without the others and each with the others is God. The one God exists in a plurality of three identifiable and distinct, not separate, persons. The three are three Gods, or three parts, or three expressions of God, but they are three persons completely united that they form the one true and eternal God. Both God the Son and God the Holy Spirit possess the attributes that can only be a true God. We have to note also that one of the three persons was ever made or created, but each one exists equal in essential being with attributes of power and glory. One God existing in three persons is made possible from all eternity reciprocal love, fellowship, the exercise of divine attributes, mutual, communion in knowledge, and interrelationship within the Godhead. Without the power of the Holy Spirit and the power of the holy word of God, Christians will not or cannot overpower, or overcome sins and temptations.

On the day of Pentecost, Jesus Christ baptized apostles and believers with the Holy Spirit, "When the day of Pentecost came, they were all together in one place. Suddenly a sound like the blowing of a violent wind came from heaven and filled the whole house where they were sitting. They saw what seemed to be tongues of fire that separated and came to rest on each of them. All of them were filled with the Holy Spirit and began to speak in other tongues as the Spirit enabled them" (Acts 2:1-4). Jesus Christ did baptize the apostles and the believers with the Holy Spirit on the day of Pentecost.

This was like in the Old Testament when the first fruits of the grain harvest were presented to God. In the same manner was the day of Pentecost, which symbolizes for the church the beginning of God's harvest for souls in the world. On the day of Pentecost, there were three manifestations of the Holy Spirit descending upon the disciples as a fulfillment of Christ promised when he said, "Do not leave Jerusalem, but wait for the gift my Father promised, which you have heard me speak about. For John baptized with water, but in a few days you will be baptized with the Holy Spirit" (Act 1:4b-5). The gift of the Father was first prophesied by the prophet Joel (Joel 2:28-29)—It is the baptism in the Holy Spirit. The fulfillment of that promise is being described as filled with the Holy Spirit. Therefore, baptized in the Spirit and filled with the Spirit are many times used interchangeably in the book of Acts. Whereas, the baptism of the Holy Spirit should not be identified with receiving the Holy Spirit at regeneration—there are distinctive works of the Holy Spirit separated by a period as the believer grows in grace and in the word of God, and in the ministry work.

Baptizing in the Holy Spirit is primarily for the preaching, teaching, healing and all other ministerial work that the Holy Spirit will be doing through the believer for the Lord. The primary purpose of the baptism in the Spirit is the receiving of power to witness for Christ so that the lost will be won. The sinners will be won over to Christ, and be taught to obey all that Christ commanded at the end, that Christ may be known, exalted, praised and the Lord and Savior of God's chosen people.

Christ told the disciples that they would receive power, something more than strength, or ability, something designated, especially power in operations, in action. The holy Spirit's power included the authority to drive out the evil spirit and the anointing to heal the sick as the two essential signs that accompany the proclamation of God's Kingdom. The baptism of the Holy Spirit power on the day of Pentecost through the believers' lives helps and moves them to witness the great boldness and power of the Holy Spirit, perform miracles, signs and wonders, heal the sick, and three thousand conversions through the preaching of the gospel of God by Apostle Peter on that day. Baptism of the Holy Spirit created a great power within. Inside all Christians then and today to personal salvation, witness with great power and proclaim the gospel of God with joy, the cross and the resurrection of our Lord and Savior.

Impartation of the Holy Spirit by Jesus Christ to the believers and disciples on the day of resurrection was different from baptism in the Spirit as experienced on the day of Pentecost. It was a new covenant experience of the disciple's regeneration and impartation of believer's new life in Christ. "And with that he breathed on them and said; receive the Holy

Spirit" (John 20:22). Regeneration of the Holy Spirit can be seen as when Christ breathed on the disciples and said receive the Holy Spirit. The Holy Spirit lived with believers and indwelled the believers, the same as when "God breathed into Adam's nostril the breath of live, and the man became a living being" (Genesis 2:7). It was the same when God told Prophet Ezekiel "Breath into the slain bones that they may live" (Ezekiel 37:9). Jesus breathed on apostles to bring them new life and to make them a new creation (2nd Corinthian 5:17), the same as when God breathed on Adam and made him a new creation.

Jesus Christ breathed on the disciples and made them a new creation in the new covenant. After Jesus Christ's resurrection, he became a life given Spirit, Christ. "I am the resurrection and I am the life" (John 11:25). When Christ breathed on the disciples, the Spirit came to them immediately, indwelled them and started a new life in them. The same is true today when a sinner confesses sin, gives their life to Christ, the Spirit indwells them and lives a new life in them. This receiving the Holy Spirit will precede the baptism in the Holy Spirit on the day of Pentecost—the baptism in the Holy Spirit was the work of the Holy Spirit in their lives. This first and second work of the Holy Spirit works in the lives of believers the same for all Christians. All believers received the Holy Spirit at the time of conversion and at another time, they will experience the baptism of the Holy Spirit for empowering them to be Jesus' witnesses for sinners and the lost. Therefore, all Christians must work hard in order to receive the Holy Spirit and be baptized in the Holy Spirit so that they can evangelize the people of the universe for our Lord and Savior Jesus Christ and also to prepare for his second coming.

Christian baptism in the Holy Spirit not only imparts believer's power to preach Jesus as Lord and Savior, but also increases the effectiveness of that witness because of strengthening and deepening relationship with the Father, Son and with the Holy Spirit. The Holy Spirit will help believers to get closer to Jesus Christ. Intimate fellowship with Jesus helps believers to have a growing desire to love, honor and please their Lord and Savior. Baptism in the Holy Spirit will help Christians to do what will bring glory to Christ not only in words but also in deeds.

They will possess Christ-like characters, love, truth and righteousness and witness to the redemptive work of Christ at all times. The baptism of the Holy Spirit is the initiation point of Spirit-filled Christians receiving the enabling power of the Holy Spirit to witness for Christ's crucified, raised, ascended into heaven and coming again boldly and clearly. Therefore, if the Holy Spirit is fully at work in the lives of believing Christians they will live in a greater conformity to Christ's holiness.

"He has filled the hungry with good things but has sent the rich away empty. He has helped his servant Israel, remembering to be merciful to Abraham and his descendants forever, even as he said to our fathers" (Luke 1:53-56). Mary's song is so good and has inspired many women in this world from generation to generation. Mary will continue to be called Blessed Mary Mother of God forever until Christ returns.

17

Christ's Life, our Life

ALL CHRISTIANS MUST BE WILLING TO GIVE UP ANY-thing that Christ asks them to give up, especially our commitment to him. The Scripture revealed when Christ was preaching, "I tell you the truth, at the renewal of all things, when the Son of Man sits on his glorious throne, you who have followed me will also sit on twelve thrones, judging the twelve tribes of Israel, and everyone who has left houses or brothers or sisters or fathers or mothers or children or fields for my sake will receive a hundred times as much and will inherit eternal life. But many who are first will be last, and many who are last will be first" (Matthew 19:28-30).

Christ's life is our life because the first are those who, because of their wealth, education, status or talents, are held in esteem by the world and sometimes by the church. The last are those who are unknown and considered unimportant in the age to come. Many who are thought to be great leaders in the church will be given positions behind others and many who were unknown will be exalted to glorious positions. This is because God the Father Almighty values people not by appearance or position, but by the sincerity, purity and love of their hearts. "When Christ who is your life, appears, then you also will appear with him in glory" (Colossians 3:4). Christ is our life. He wants us to live holy lives. This is an essential part of work of redemption in Christ. It is with the fellowship communion that the love for Jesus Christ's Christians must maintain personal communion with Christ. Christ must be the center of all Christian activities.

Christ's life believers will set their minds, spirits, souls and bodies on Christ because their lives are in Christ who is seated in heaven at the right hand of God. Christians must let their attitudes be determined by things above. They must evaluate and view everything based on an eternal and heavenly perspective. Christian goals and purposes must be based and centered on Jesus; they must resist any form of sin at all times in everything they do. Christians must be clothed with Christ's life, Spiritual graces, the power of the Holy Spirit with the experiences and blessings that are with Christ in heaven, which he will give to those who love him and with sincere heart seek him diligently and pursue his holiness with all their hearts.

Christ's life is the life of those who believe in him. Follow him and obey his commands sincerely. When Christ's life is the life of Christians, the believer will continually read the word of God, study the word of God, mediate on the word of God and pray for everything needed until they receive it. They pray until Christ richly dwells in them by his Spirit. When this is manifest in the lives of believers their thoughts, words, deeds and motivations will be influenced and controlled by Jesus Christ from above through the power of his Spirit.

Christians will be singing and praising the Lord. When Christ is our life, the Christian will be able to say with confidence, "I have fought the good fight, I have finished the race, I have kept the faith; now there is in store for me the crown of righteousness, which the Lord, the righteous judge, will award to me on that day and not only to me, but also to all who have longed for his appearing" (2nd Timothy 4:7-8). When Christ is our life, we do everything in his holy name, witnessing, preaching and praying all in his holy name. Christian ministry life is from Christ and for Christ. Christian life is a life well devoted to our Lord and Savior. Christian life is a life of the good fight, the fight against all the principalities and power of evil, the fight against Satan and his demonic power and evil spirit. Christians fight against the power of this dark world and spiritual forces of evil in the heavenly realm.

In spite of all these, Christians who remain faithful to Christ will receive a reward, many rewards and a crown of righteousness to all who remain faithful and loyal to Jesus Christ to the end. Especially all Christians who were waiting for Christ's second coming, God has reserved many rewards in heaven for those who serve him faithfully on this earth. When Christ was crucified believers were also crucified. When Christ was persecuted Christians were persecuted. When Christ was dead, Christians died. When Christ was raised from the dead Christians were raised from the dead. Christ's resurrection is the resurrection of all Christians. Christ's life is the life of Christians. Without Christ, there is no life for Christians.

"His father Zechariah was filled with the Holy Spirit and prophesied: Praise be to the Lord, the God of Israel, because he has come and has redeemed his people, He has raised up a horn of salvation for us in the house of his servant David" (Luke 1:67-69). At that moment in Zechariah's life the Holy Spirit empowered him. The same is true with many prophets, important people who were associated with the birth of Christ. Through Christ's ascension to heaven, the way was opened for all Christians to be filled with the Holy Spirit.

18

Christ at the Right Hand of God

THE SCRIPTURE REVEALED THAT CHRIST IS SITTING AT the right hand of God, "The Son is the radiance of God's glory and the exact representation of his being, sustaining all things, by his powerful word" (Hebrews 1:3). Christ Jesus our Lord and Savior provided people of this universe with the gifts of grace and salvation, his atoning sacrifice and resurrection whereby all Christians are reconciled to God. He took his place of authority and sat down at the right hand of God the Father Almighty. Christ's redeeming love and activities in heaven involve the ministry of advocate and mediator of a new covenant. Christ is our great intercessor in heaven and baptizer of the Holy Spirit.

Christ is superior to all the prophets from the Old Testament and Christ is superior to all the angels in heaven because Christ is the true Son of God. "For every house is built by someone, but God is the builder of everything. Moses was faithful as a servant in all God's house, testifying to what would be said in future. However, Christ is faithful in his own house as the Son of God. And we are his house, if we hold on to our courage and the hope of which we boast" (Hebrews 3:4-6). Jesus Christ is the Son of God and superior to Moses; Jesus is faithful in his own house as the Son of God. This part of the book of Hebrews scripture warns and exhorts those who belong to Christ. It indicates that salvation is conditional and it requires a persevering faith in the Lord Jesus Christ. God's grace was made possible through Christians' saving faith relationship in Jesus Christ, which also made the grace of God sufficient for sustaining the salvation of God.

Christian security is maintained as long as they abide in Christ in loving obedience to him. "To which of the angels did God ever say sit at my right hand until I make your enemies a footstool for your feet" (Hebrews 1:13). Jesus Christ is superior to the angels because Christ Jesus is the Son of God and he is seated at the right hand of God. Jesus Christ is God's Son who radiates God's glory because he shares God's nature and essence. Whatever God the Father almighty is in his character, attributes and nature, Jesus Christ is the exact and the same representation. Therefore, God himself exalted him, "that at the name of Jesus every knee should bow, in heaven and on earth and under the earth, and every the tongue confess that Jesus Christ is Lord, to the glory of God the Father" (Philippians 2:10-11). God's revelation of himself is no longer fragmentary and no longer incomplete, as in Old Testament times. Jesus Christ, the Son, is the revelation of the Father. He is full, complete and clearly known. "Christ is the image of the invisible God, the first-born over all creations. For by him all things were created things in heaven and things on earth, visible and invisible, whether thrones or powers or rulers or authorities; all this were created by him and for him" (Colossians 1:15-16).

Christ is supreme over any created being. He is the first-born, heir and ruler of all creations. He is the eternal Son. All things in heaven and on earth, material things physical or spiritual, owe their existence to Jesus Christ's work as the active agent in creation. All things were held together and all things were sustained by him and for him. On the day of resurrection Jesus Christ became the head of the church, the blessed ruler of all human souls on earth. Jesus Christ was the first-born among the dead. This implies the subsequent reservation of all those for whom he died.

The Scripture continues, "But because of his great love for us, God, who is rich in mercy, made us alive with Christ even when we were dead in transgressions it is by grace you have been saved. And God raised us up, in the heavenly realms in Christ Jesus (Ephesians 2:4-6). All Christians are one in him as he is one with the Father. When Jesus Christ was raised we were raised with him. Moreover, God made all Christians to be seated with Christ in heaven. Jesus Christ has done a great thing for all those who believe in him and committed their lives to Christ. Holy is his name forever—we are seated where Christ sits at the right hand of God.

"Since, then, you have been raised with Christ, set your hearts on things above, where Christ is seated at the right hand of God set your minds on things above not on earthly things" (Colossians 3:1-2). Our lives are in Jesus Christ who is seated in heaven. We must set our minds and let our attitudes be determined by things above. We must set our minds on, view and evaluate everything in our life according to the eternal and heavenly perspective. Our goal in life must be centered on Christ Jesus who alone is seated at the right hand of God. Christians must resist sins and all the worldly lusts that contaminate the body, spirit and soul, continuously focus on Jesus Christ, and wait earnestly for his return.

"After The Lord Jesus had spoken to them, he was taken up into heaven and he sat at the right hand of God" (Mark 16:19). Our lord and savior Jesus Christ will continue to sit at the right hand of God, interceding for his people and the people of the world, sending all Christians to the sinners and the lost, telling them to repent because the kingdom of God is at hand. He did not want anyone to perish. He wants them to come to the knowledge of repentance and pray for forgiveness of sin, which is only in him. Christ listens and answers believer's prayers if he knows that what they ask for is good for them. His answer to prayers can be to wait, that it is not yet time, or he has something better than what you ask for from him. Christ as our advocate in heaven, advocating the Father of a new covenant, is our prophet and priest of a new covenant. He will save all those who will come to him. By faith come you sinners and the lost. He is waiting for you at the right hand of God.

"*(As he said through his holy prophets of long ago). Salvation from our enemies and from the hand of all who hate us—to show mercy to our fathers and to remember his holy covenant, the oath he swore to our father Abraham*" *(Luke 1:70-73).* Zechariah's song opened his heart to the salvation of God the Father through God the Son, and he revealed the promise of God, which was spoken by His prophets in ages past.

19

Christ, our King of Kings

THE SCRIPTURE REVEALED TO US HOW OUR LORD JESUS Christ is our King of kings, "Now to the King Eternal, Immortal, Invisible, the only God, be honor and glory for ever and ever, amen" (1st Timothy 1:17). Jesus Christ is the believers' King of kings. Believing in him and serving him, he will displace his mercy and unlimited patience to many others who will hear our testimony and believe in the goodness of the Lord, and be saved so that God the Almighty's abundant grace and mercy toward all Christians might encourage the sinners and the lust to be saved and the gospel to be preached to them, the gospel to be preached to the idol worshipers, pagans and all other people of various, different religions in the world, even to the darkest heart, who has never seen the light of God will be converted. Christians will be confidently present. The gospel and the power of the Spirit of God will manifest on all those who hear the gospel preach to them.

The Scripture revealed Paul sent his letter to Timothy and he said, "In the sight of God, who gives life to everything, and of Christ Jesus, who while testifying before Pontius Pilate made the good confession, I charge you to keep this command without spot or blame until the appearing of our Lord Jesus

Christ, which God will bring about in his own time God the blessed and only Ruler, the King of kings and the Lord of lords, who alone is immortal and who lives in unapproachable light, whom no one has seen or can see to him be honor and might forever amen" (1ˢᵗ Timothy 6:13-16). All Christians must stand firm in the faith. They should not allow anything to move them in no matter what occupation God has placed them; Christians must be immovable and steadfast in the Lord.

All believers should be encouraged and full of joy waiting for Christ appearing on the air. Loving the Lord Jesus Christ and longing for his return and his immediate presence in the life of all Christians must be a basic motivation in our lives. "For my thoughts are not your thoughts, neither are your ways my ways declares the Lord. As the heavens are higher than the earth, so are my ways higher than your ways and my thoughts than your thoughts" (Isaiah 55:8-9). This Scripture is telling us that God's thoughts and God's ways are not the same as those of natural people. God said that human minds and hearts could be renewed and transformed by seeking him, the giver of lives. Therefore, our thoughts and ways will begin to conform to his ways. A believer's greatest desire should be to live in good harmony and conformity to the likeness of our Lord so that everything we are doing will be pleasing in the sight of God.

Christians who wanted to please the Lord must be abiding in his word as well as responding to the Holy Spirit's leading. God must not be placed on the same level with any human being or any other being that he created. God's existence is in a totally different realm. He dwells in perfect and pure existence, far above any other creations. God wants believers to know that he is God. There is no other beside him. He will always be God of all creations and all Christians must depend on him as the creator, now and forever.

The Lord Jesus Christ is the King of kings the Scripture says, "I looked and there before me was a white cloud, and seated on the cloud was one like a Son of man with a crown of gold on his head and a sharp sickle in his hand" (Revelation 14:14). Our Lord Jesus Christ himself initiates the reaping of the earth's harvest. "You will be for me a kingdom of priests and a holy nation. These are the words you are to speak to the Israelites" (Exodus 19:6). As part of God's covenant purpose for the Israelites after bringing them out of Egypt, they were to be a kingdom of priests set apart and consecrated for the work of the Lord. In the same way today, our Lord and Savior redeemed us from our sins and bought us with his precious blood in order for us to be able to serve the Lord. Believers in a new covenant, we are called the kingdom of priests.

All Christians must obey King Jesus, "Do not be in a hurry to leave the king's presence. Do not stand up for a bad cause, for he will do whatever he pleases. Since a king's word is supreme, who can say to him, 'What are you doing?'" (Ecclesiastes 8:3-4). Obedience is the key to serve the Lord; Christians must follow his commandment and be obedient to his word. All Christians must obey King Jesus' commands. Christians must obey the law of governments, kings and rulers. "The king's heart is in the hand of the Lord; he directs it like water" (Proverbs 21:1). God Almighty has the power and authority over all the rulers of the world and at times, he chooses to influence their decisions so as to further his work of redemption and purpose for our lives.

The emphasis is that through Christian prayers and praise of God's people, God will answer the prayer of believers to influence the people of the world. Prayers of God's people might influence the Lord to direct the decisions of the rulers of this earth fully in accordance to God's will. God Almighty

Father, Son and Holy Spirit, wants his people to be righteous and just rather than merely involved in religious activities. Praise, worship and offerings are unacceptable to God if Christians are not living rightly. Gifts offered to God should and must be accompanied by holy lives; otherwise, they are not acceptable to God in Christ. Jesus Christ is the King of kings. He is the believer's King forever. His kingdom will have no end.

"To rescue us from the hand of our enemies and to enable us to serve him without fear in holiness and righteousness before him all our days. And you, my child, will be called a prophet of the Most High; for you will go on before the Lord to prepare the way for him" (Luke 1:72-76). The ultimate objective of our redemption is to be delivered from our enemies, in order to serve God in holiness and righteousness before him all our days.

20

Christ Jesus the Messiah

JESUS CHRIST IS OUR BLESSED MESSIAH. THE SCRIPTURE revealed again and again that Christ is the awaiting expected Messiah of the people of Israel. From the Old Testament to the New Testament, the Scripture clearly stated that Christ is the Messiah. There are many prophesies from the prophets concerning Jesus Christ being the Messiah. "Therefore the Lord himself will give you a sign: the virgin will be with child and will give birth to a son and will call him Immanuel" (Isaiah 7:14). Prophet Isaiah prophesied about the coming of the Messiah. He said the misery of the beginning of the Messiah is that a virgin sign, a new unmarried woman, will be pregnant; this prophesy was fulfilled when Christ was born by the Virgin Mary. Mary was a virgin and remains a virgin until the birth of Jesus Christ. The conception was through the Holy Spirit and God the Father Almighty who spoke Christ into the womb of Mary through the power of his Spirit, because God Almighty said, "not by my power but by my Spirit"

Christ is the one and only Son of God. He was called Immanuel, God with us, God in us. "The Scepter will not depart from Judah, nor the ruler's staff from between his feet, until he comes to whom it belongs and the obedience of the nations is his" (Genesis 49:10). The blessing conferred on Judah indicates that he was given the rights of the first-born, and therefore, the blessing promised to Abraham. The fact is that all nations will be blessed through him by the offspring of the woman's birth.

This ultimately refers to the coming of the Messiah, Jesus Christ, who came through the line of Judah. Jacob prophesied that all people on earth would obey him and he would bring great spiritual blessings. Jesus Christ is the blessed Messiah. Those who believe in him will have life in him. "I will place shepherds over them, who will tend them, and will no longer be afraid or terrified, nor will any be afraid or terrified, nor will any be missing, declares the Lord. The days are coming, declares the Lord, when I will raise up to David a righteous Branch" (Jeremiah 23:4-5). This prophesy also points to the Messiah Jesus Christ. Christ is the David seed, born in Bethlehem of Judea. "Jesus spoke all these things to the crowed in parables he did not say anything to them without using a parable. So was fulfilled what was speaking through the prophets: I will open my mouth in parables, I will utter things hidden since the creation of the world" (Matthew 13:34). The gospel and the true believers will be planted all over the world. Parables are storms from everyday life that relate and that illustrate certain spiritual truths; consequences are found in revealing truth to those who are spiritual while at the same time concealing them from non-Christians or nonbelievers.

As the Scripture has already said, the Messiah will speak in parables. This is part of the proof that the Messiah is truly Jesus Christ. "Rejoiced greatly, O Daughter of Zion, shout Daughter of Jerusalem see, your King comes to you, righteous and having salvation, gentle and riding on a donkey on a colt, the foal of a donkey" (Zechariah 9:9). At the end or toward the end of his ministry, Jesus Christ the Messiah rode on a donkey to Jerusalem a week before his crucifixion. Jesus Christ is our King and he is the King of kings. It was a great rejoicing and is still a great rejoicing today. There is a greater cause for rejoicing because Christ is the coming King, not in royal splendor but in humility.

The prophet Zechariah's prophesy was fulfilled by Jesus Christ a week before his crucifixion. Zechariah's prophesy foresees Jesus' triumphal entry into Jerusalem by riding on a donkey into the holy city. In this way, Jesus Christ declared himself to be the Messiah and Savior Lord. "As he approached Jerusalem and saw the city, he wept over it and said. If you, even you, had only known on this day what would bring peace but now it is hidden from your eyes" (Luke 19:41-42). Our Lord Jesus, knew that the people of Israel's ruling council and the rulers and leaders were expecting a political Messiah who would come, liberate and deliver them from the Roman Empire. He knows they will surely rejected him because that is the type of Messiah they are waiting for or expecting.

They rejected Jesus Christ as God's promised Messiah; Christ wept in pity, sorry for the people who would soon suffer judgment. Christ lamented, heavy of burden, crying of the soul in agony. Our Lord and Savior God the Son reveals not only his own feelings but also God's broken heart over the lost, sinners, the entire human race and the people of Israel, their refusal to repent from their sin and accept the gift of salvation. "Those who went ahead and those who followed shouted. Hosanna—blessed is he who comes in the name of the Lord. Blessed is the coming kingdom of our father David Hosanna in the highest" (Mark 11:9). The crowd believed that the Messiah would restore Israel nationally and rule the nations politically. They failed to understand the purpose that Jesus Christ expressed regarding his coming into the world.

The following week, the same crowd shouted, "Crucify him," when they thought he was not the Messiah they were waiting for. God the Father knows that Christ is the Messiah. All those who believe in Jesus Christ know that he is the promised Messiah. Believe in him; you will have life in him, life everlasting. "They divide my garments among them and cast lots for my clothing" (Psalm 22:18). This prophesy was fulfilled when Christ was crucified. This is a very valuable prophetic reference that shows clearly that Christ Jesus is the promised Messiah.

The Samaritan woman recognized the Messiah. She ran to the village and announced to all the people in her village, "When a Samaritan woman came to draw water, Jesus said to her, will you give me a drink? Sir, the woman said, I can see that you are a prophet. Our Father worshiped on this mountain, but you Jews claim that the place where we must worship is in Jerusalem. The woman said I know that Messiah called Christ is coming. When he comes, he will explain everything to us. Then Jesus declared, I who speak to you am he" (John 4:7, 19, 25-26). The Samaritan woman engaged in a conversation with Jesus. The woman opened up her heart to the Lord and Jesus Christ revealed the truth to her, his commitment to his heavenly Father, his Father's purpose and Christ's desire to bring the eternal life to the Samaritan woman.

Jesus Christ came to the world to save sinners and the lost. This goal is more important to him than food and drink. Christians must follow the example of our Lord. People from rural areas of the world must listen and hear the gospel of God and the word of God; Christians must find any opportunity and way to speak and share to the people about the gift of salvation and their spiritual need and those who want to know about Jesus.

The water that Jesus offered the Samaritan woman is spiritual, like drinking the water of life requires regular communion with the source of the living water, which is Jesus Christ himself. It is a progressive action, whereby Christians will continuously drink the water of life as long as they abide in Christ. Jesus Christ teaches, "A time is and his now come when the true worshiper will worship the Father in Spirit and in truth" (John 4:23). Christians will worship in spirit, which means the level at which true worship occurs, where the worshipers' spirit connects with the Spirit of God. When a person comes to God in complete sincerity and with the spirit that is directed by the life and activity of the Holy Spirit, he or she will receive the life of Christ.

A Christian must maintain a Christ-like character, intrinsic to the Holy Spirit and especially the believer must worship at the heart of the gospel. Christian worship must take place according to the truth of God the Father that is revealed in his Son and received through the Spirit. Worship in truth means because Jesus Christ is the truth, to live in union with Jesus Christ requires speaking the truth with love. Whereas, untrue Christians remain in deception and darkness and they can be outside the kingdom of heaven. "Then living her water jar, the woman went back to the town and said to the people come, see a man who told me everything I ever did. Could this be the Christ? (John 4:29). The woman shares her finding knowledge of the Messiah with the people in her town.

Christians who bring other people to saving faith in Christ are doing something of eternal consequence. They will one day rejoice in heaven over those who are saved through their preaching and teaching of prayers and witnesses. They must also understand that their work is often a reaping of the labor of others and the power of the Holy Spirit. Jesus Christ revealed himself to the Samaritan woman that he is the awaiting and coming Messiah of the people of Israel and of the world.

"To give his people the knowledge of salvation through the forgiveness of their sins, because of the tender mercy of our God, by which the rising sun will come to us from heaven to shine on those living in darkness and in the shadow of death, to guide our feet into the path of peace" (Luke 1:77-79). The birth of the Savior, which is the greatest event in all history, occurred in the most humble circumstances.

21

Christ Jesus our Shepherd

JESUS CHRIST IS THE SHEPHERD OF THE SHEEP. THE SCRIP-ture revealed in the Old Testament and New Testament, "The Lord is my shepherd; I shall not be in want. He makes me to lie down in green pastures he leads me beside quiet waters, he restores my soul. He guides me in paths of righteousness for his name's sake. Surely goodness and love will follow me all the days of my life, and I will dwell in the house of the Lord forever" (Psalm 23:1-3, 6). The Scripture revealed that on the road to Bethlehem there is a well with a stone coping around it. Next to it is a shepherd's large stone hollowed out to hold thirty or forty gallons of water for the sheep to drink.

In this popular song of David, he was talking about a shepherd's cup, which overflows because of God's blessings that are rushing into it. "Now he had to go through Samaria called Sychar, near the plot of ground Jacob had given to his son Joseph. Jacob's well was there, and Jesus, tired as he was from the journey, sat down by the well. It was about the sixth hour" (John 4:4). This is more proof that says Christ is a shepherd of the sheep. Jesus answered, "Everyone who drinks this water will be thirsty again, but whoever drinks the water I give him will never thirst, indeed, the water I give him will became in him a spring of water welling up to eternal life" (John 4:13-14). Sitting down by the well in order to fill the thirsty heart with the living, spring of water, burbling up to eternal life, water that is welling up to eternal life, free living water. Christ came to this world to give the water of life to those who are hungry and thirsty for righteousness, spring water to the sinners and to all his lost sheep so that they will never be thirsty anymore.

Jesus Christ our Lord and Savior is our shepherd. God compares himself to a shepherd in order to illustrate his great love for his people. Our Lord Jesus Christ, "Save your people and bless your inheritance; be their shepherd and carry them forever" (Psalm 28:9). A faithful believer of Jesus Christ may feel that God is too far away or not listening to his or her prayers. This experience does not last as long as a believer continues to draw near to God through Jesus Christ. After the believer have suffered a while, or has gone through the trial, the Lord will stretch his holy hands in response to the trouble and help the sheep because a shepherd cares for his sheep.

As the Scripture said, "He tends his flock like a shepherd; he gathers the Lambs in his arms and carries them close to his heart; he gently leads those that have young" (Isaiah 40:11). God was described as one who picks up individual believers like a Lamb in order to protect them, guide them and carry them close to his heart. Even though God is all-powerful and all merciful, he still cares for all those who belong to him, and those who have a personal relationship with him. Christians must never think that God is so powerful and uncompassionate that he ignores the needs, troubles and problems of every Christian. We also applied this psalm to all the New Testament believers, "For he is our God and we are the people of his pasture, the flock under his care" (Psalm 95:7). Christ is our shepherd. "Then we your people, the sheep of your pasture, will praise you forever, from generation to generation we will recount your praises" (Psalm 79:13). The true emphasis is that God, through Jesus Christ and by the Holy Spirit, is concerned about each of his children and he is near every one of his children, just as a good shepherd is for his sheep.

Christians are the Lord's sheep. Christians belong to the Lord and they are the special objects of his affection and attention. When we stray away, or are lost, the Lord always takes time to redeem us with his shed precious blood and Christians now belong to the good shepherd. As a believer and as his sheep we can claim the promises when believers respond to his voice and follow him. Christians will not lack anything for the will of God will be accomplish in every individual Christians' life, even in times of hardship, because they trust in his love and his commitment for them.

In the presence and the nearness of the shepherd the sheep can lie down in peace without worry of wolf by day or by night; they are free from fear, from worry because of the power of the indwelling of the Holy Spirit as their comforter, counselor and helper who is communicating Christ's shepherd care and presence to them. Christians confidently rest on the presence of Jesus Christ in the green pasture—Jesus Christ is the word of God, which is required and necessary for an abundant life.

The Holy Spirit leads Christians beside Christ's quiet waters, the water of eternal life. When individual Christians get discouraged as sheep, the good shepherd revives and reenergizes their soul through the power and grace. He guides believers by the Spirit of God, in their chosen paths, of God's way of holiness. Christians must follow the shepherd with the Spirit of obedience by listening to the shepherd's voice, "A stranger they will not follow or they will not listen to strangers' voice" (John 10:5). In the time of danger, hardship, trouble, tribulations, persecutions and death, the sheep will not fear any evil because the shepherd is with them in every way and in all their lives.

God will strengthened the sheep with his power and authority. God's rod and staff reassure the sheep of the shepherds' love and protection in their lives. In the midst of all the evil forces that confronted the sheep the shepherd is always there to deliver them. God provided his people with sufficient grace to live and rejoice in his presence. Christians will eat at the Lord's table by faith, thanksgiving and hope, fully in peace and fully protected by the blood of the shepherd and the broken body of the good shepherd.

God's special favor and the power of anointing of the Holy Spirit will continuously rush blessings to the believer's spirit, soul and body. The shepherd will continue to accompany the sheep through life's journey. They will receive constant grace, help, kindness, favor and support. No matter what happens they can trust the good shepherd to work all things for their good. The goal of the sheep following the shepherd and experiencing his goodness and love and mercy is that one day they are going to be with the Lord to see his face and serve him forever in his house.

"I am the good shepherd; the good shepherd lays down his life for the sheep. The hired hands are not the shepherd who owns the sheep. Therefore, when he sees the wolf coming, he abandons the sheep. He runs away because he is a hired hand and cares nothing for the sheep. I am the good shepherd; I know my sheep and my sheep know me—just as the Father knows me and I know the Father—and I lay down my life for the sheep. I have other sheep that are not of this sheep pen. I must bring them also. They too will listen to my voice, and there shall be one flock and one shepherd." (John 10:11-16) Our Lord Jesus Christ declared himself the Father's promised good shepherd, which illustrated Jesus Christ's tenderness, devotion, care and love for those who come to him by faith.

Jesus loves and cares for all who believe in him as a good shepherd tenderly cares for his sheep. The difference of Christ's good shepherd is that of his willingness to die for his sheep. This emphasizes the uniqueness of Jesus Christ as the shepherd; his death on the cross saves his sheep from eternal death. Christ is called the great shepherd, "May the God of peace, who through the blood of the eternal covenant brought back from the dead our Lord Jesus, that great shepherd of the sheep" (Hebrews 13:20). In addition, our Lord was called the Chief Shepherd, "And when the Chief shepherd appears, you will receive the crown of glory that will never face away" (1st Peter 5:4). Christians must be aware that the pastor, reverend or minister who services merely to earn a living or to gain honor is like the hired hand he is not the true shepherd. The true pastors, ministers and reverends who care for their sheep, the congregation members of their church, are the good shepherds. False preachers, pastors and ministers think first of themselves and their position, how they can use it to rob the people of their church. They use their position through those members who disagree with them in some of their ungodly issues and plans.

The Lord Jesus Christ is telling us that God's knowledge and his love for his children involve personal affection, faithfulness and constant providential care. God upholds his own with his holy hands. Christians are never out of God's mind and God continually watches over them with his holy eye for their own good. Those who are the true sheep of Jesus Christ obey his voice and follow him as well as being in constant fellowship with the shepherd. The sheep listens to the voice of the shepherd and follow his command. Those who are following the shepherd receive eternal life. Those who stray from the shepherd and refuse to listen prove that they are not his sheep.

Jesus Christ is the shepherd of the sheep believing in him. Your sins according to the Scripture, "If we confess our sins, he is faithful and just and will forgive us our sins and purify us from all unrighteousness" (1st John 1:9). All Christians must admit their sins, confess them and seek forgiveness and purification from God. Two things happen when Christians or sinners and nonbelievers confesses their sins; they will receive forgiveness and reconciliation with God. They will be made pure. God will purify them from any filthiness, removal of the guilt of sins and the destruction of sin's power will be removed so that they can live holy lives.

The Scripture says, "And this is the testimony: God has given us eternal life, and this life is in his Son. He who has the Son has life; He who does not have the Son of God does not have life. I write these things to you who believe in the name of the Son of God so that you may know that you have eternal life" (1st John 5:11-13). John declares that the reason why he wrote his letter was to make it clear to all the believers and all people that the eternal life that God provided is only in his Son Jesus Christ. All the people in this world must hear the gospel of God preached to them because eternal life is in God the Son, who is the Lord Jesus Christ. It cannot and it can never be received or possessed in any other way. "Jesus Christ is the way, the truth and the life" (John 14:6). Eternal life is the life of Jesus Christ in all believers. Christians will have eternal life as long as they maintain a vital faithful relationship with Christ.

John provided Christians with Spirit to inspire authoritative assurance of faith and the gift of grace and salvation. This is the reason why there is no other shepherd who cared for the sheep than Jesus Christ the great shepherd, the good shepherd, and the Chief shepherd of all the sheep in the universe. Give your life to the good shepherd today, follow him, listen to him, commit your life into his holy hand, obey his command, surrender your lives to him. He will take good care of the sheep.

Make sure that nothing separates you from him, "Who shall separate us from the love of Christ? Shall trouble or hardship or persecution or famine or nakedness or danger or sword? As it is written: for your sake, we face death all day long; we are considered as sheep to be slaughtered. No, in all these things we are more than conquerors through him who loved us. For I am convinced that neither death nor life, neither angels nor demons, neither the present nor the future, nor any powers, neither height, not depth, nor anything else in all creation, will be able to separate us from the love of God that is in Christ Jesus our Lord" (Romans 8:35-39). All the adversities that Apostle Paul mentioned have been a plague for all the people of God from generation to generation. Christians should not think it strange or lose hope if they experience persecution, poverty, hunger, afflictions or tribulations or if they are in any danger. They should know that when all these things happened it does not mean that God the Father, God the Son and God the Holy Spirit have forsaken them, or have stopped loving them.

Believing Christian sufferings increases God's love and blessings, and comfort, God the Holy Spirit is the comforter; he will comfort his people. Christians will overcome through Christ's unfailing love; if anyone fails in their spiritual life and stops walking with the Lord, it is because of their own disobedience and neglect to remain in Christ. Only in Christ Jesus is God's love revealed to his people and only in Christ Jesus do people experience the love of Christ. Christians must remain in Christ and make him their Lord and Savior so that they can have the certainty that will never be separated from the Love of God, which is in Christ Jesus our Lord. Jesus Christ is the Good shepherd, the Great shepherd, and the Chief shepherd. Surrender your life to him; you will have eternal life in him.

"And there were shepherds living out in the fields nearby, keeping watch over their flocks at night. An angel of the Lord appeared to them, and the glory of the Lord shone around them, and they were terrified. But the angel said to them, "Do not be afraid. I bring you good news of great joy that will be for all the people" (Luke 2:8-10). Jesus Christ was called a Savior by angels at his birth. As a Savior, Christ has come to deliver all the people of this world from their sins, Satan's domain, the ungodly world, fear and death.

22

Christian Thankfulness for God's Divine Activities

G OD THE FATHER ALMIGHTY, THE COMPASSIONATE and gracious God, all powerful, all knowing, all merciful and mighty, who is full of truth and righteousness, abounding in loving kindness, mercy and love. Our God has complete knowledge of everyone in the universe. All our thoughts and our actions are naked, open before him. It is always good and rewarding to meditate on God's divine truths and wills for our lives and apply it to ourselves in all the areas of our lives.

Believers should learn and practice how to lift their hearts up in prayer to the Lord instead of occupying our mind with unprofitable, unfriendly and unloving things. As we know is that God is the all-knowing of all things. He is omniscient. He is omnipresent; meaning that he is everywhere at all times. His truths must be acknowledged by all the people in the world. God, who takes notice of every step we make, every right or wrong steps we take, is the ruler of souls of human beings. He knows which step and walk we walk either toward him or far away from him.

God knows when we move away from him and follow or keep bad company. He knows what is in every human heart either we belongs to him or we belong to any ritual things of this world. There is not a word that we spoke that he does not know how the thought came to us and what way we uttered it.

Wherever we are, whatever we are doing, we are under the loving and controlling eye and the hand of God. We cannot know how God searches or by what means he sees us wherever we may be. We are in his garden. If we who believe in him should think about this as well as those who say there is no God, they will stay away from evil and think no evil against each other.

People of this world should know that someone is watching over them every step of the way. As long as we are still in this tent, which means this body that our soul lives in, we cannot see God, but God sees us perfectly every time. There is nothing, nothing can hide us from the Almighty God, no clothes, no darkness. There is no form of disguise that can hide us from God. He is the creator of heaven and earth and everything that he created. Obey him, and he uses them as instruments to carry out his purposes.

The light cannot hide us. He sees through the greatest light. He created the light. We believers must be very happy and rejoice because nothing can remove us from the sustaining hand of God and comforting presence of the Almighty God. Even if a believer is persecuted, killed, his soul will ascend to heaven and live with Christ forever.

Nothing can separate him or her from the love of Jesus Christ the Savior who will raise the persecuted Christian's body a glorious body. Nothing can separate believers from their Lord. Believers are always happy doing the service of the Lord by exercising strong faith, hope and with prayers, Jesus Christ is the rock of salvation of those who believe in him.

Hallelujah, because of him, through him, and to him are all things that pertain to this world and knowledge, comfort, health, safety, progress, power and usefulness.

Let all his creations bless his Holy Name. Our primary goal on this earth is to bless the Lord. The earth is full of his praises and thankfulness. The sand at the Sea shore, the flowers, the insects, animals, birds of the air, mountains, rivers, trees clouds, Sun, moon, stars all the eight planets from this earth to Pluto, all must give his praise that is due him.

All the people of this earth young and old, children, babies, household pets, must give unceasing praise to God. All the servants of God, all the people of God must give him the praise that is due him. All places of his dominion must praise his Holy name. Everything on earth and under the earth must praise his Holy name. Let all the ministers, pastors, reverends and or-dained ministers preach and teach the true gospel that will make the heart of people open and give themselves to the Al-mighty God.

Let them seek, knock, ask and pray to God in spirit and in truth forever and forever. The Spirit says, come Lord Jesus.

"Suddenly a great company of the heavenly host appeared with the angle, praising God and saying, Glory to God in the highest, and on earth peace to men on whom his favor rests" (Luke 2:13-14). Christ has been anointed as the Messiah of God and the Lord who rules over his people and the people of the world.

Summary

JESUS CHRIST IS THE LIFE OF ALL THOSE WHO BELIEVE IN him; Christ's life can never be compared to any life on earth. Life without God is empty and has no meaning. Immediately, when a sinner gives his or her life to Jesus Christ, he or she begins a new life in Christ. Life in Christ is a life of total surrender to his Lordship, total commitment to his word, total obedience to his command. Christ becomes the controller, the director, the sustainer of believers' lives.

Christ sent the Holy Spirit to dwell in the heart of the believers; a new Spirit, a new heat, a new name were given to those who totally and willingly surrendered to the Lordship of Christ, who give their life to Jesus Christ. The believers became a new creature; the believer receives supernatural manifestation of the Holy Spirit. This manifestation of the Holy Spirit is given for the building and sanctifying of the believers. Helping them to live Christian lives; without the empowerment of the Holy Spirit believers cannot live Christian lives, lives that God requires, which is the life of holiness. These spiritual gifts are the same for all Christians all over the world. Christian believers will receive the power, ability and great wisdom to witness to the sinners and the lost, to tell others about the gift of grace and salvation, which is in Christ Jesus our Lord. This manifestation of the Holy Spirit to believers is given according to the Spirit will according to the need of the believers. Christians must desire the gift of the Holy Spirit. Some believers may have more than one gift, according to his or her ability. We can say that Christian life in Jesus Christ is life in the Spirit.

It is a life that the Spirit of God controls, directs and helps to grow. Christian life in Jesus Christ must be a life of obedience. Without obedience no one can serve the Lord accurately and sincerely. Some Christians speak in tongues and utterance inspired by the Holy Spirit that reveals knowledge about people, circumstances and Biblical truth. The speaking in tongues is usually connected with prophesies. Life in Jesus Christ is a life of faith in Jesus Christ, faith alone in Christ alone. This is a supernatural faith that is imparted by the Holy Spirit that helps and enables Christians to believe in God's extraordinary and miraculous miracles. It is a faith that can move mountains; it is a faith that can be found in other manifestations such as healings, visions and miracles.

Christian life in Christ is the life of love. Our Lord Jesus Christ said love your neighbor, love your enemy; Christ's life in Christian lives is characterized with love. Speaking in tongues involves the human spirit and the Spirit of God intermingling that the Christian believers will communicate directly to God in prayer, in praising the Lord, in blessings and in given thankfulness to God. Praying in tongues by giving expression or utterance at the level where a believer's spirit rather than his or her mind, praying for oneself, or praying for others under the direction and influence of the Holy Spirit apart from the activity of the believer's mind. To make it clearer, speaking in tongues a believer speaks primarily to God and not to human beings. The tongues are directed to God, the believer communes with God by the Holy Spirit. What is spoken are mysteries and are things that are not understandable to the believer or the hearer.

Christian life in Christ is the life of joy unspeakable in the Holy Spirit. Christian life in Christ is a life of new creation through the creative command of God. "Therefore, if anyone is in Christ, he is a new creation; the old has gone, the new has come! All this is from God, who reconciled us to himself through Christ and gave us the ministry of reconciliation that

God was reconciling the world to himself in Christ, not counting men's sins against them. Moreover, he has committed to us the message of reconciliation. We are therefore Christ's ambassadors, as though God were making his appeal through us. We implore you on Christ's behalf: be reconciled to God" (2nd Corinthians 5:17-20). Reconciliation becomes effective for each individual Christian through their personal repentance and faith in Jesus Christ. Reconciliation is one of the aspects of the work of Jesus Christ, redemptive work, where a sinner is restored and fellowship with God, through Jesus Christ's atoning death, God the Father has removed the barrier of sin and he has opened a way for the sinner to return to him.

A Christian becomes a new person, renewed after God's image, sharing God's glory with a renewed knowledge, wisdom and understanding, as well as living a life of holiness that God Almighty requires from every people in the world.

The life of Jesus Christ in the life of believing Christians is not a boring life, there is no dull moment for the children of God; the believing Christians because Christ's life is a life of missionary journey going from one village to another village, from one town to another town, from one city to another city, from one country to another country. Telling the unsafe sinners, those who have never heard about Jesus, the good news of the gospel of God. The life of Jesus Christ in the life of believing Christians is a life of children's ministry telling the children about the love of Jesus, the story of Jesus when he was a baby, and when he was growing up like them.

The life of Jesus Christ in the life of believing Christians is the life of youth ministry leading young adults to him, telling them how to live in peace with their fellow young adult in their neighborhood, in their school and in their community. The Life of Jesus Christ in the life of believing Christians is the life of college campus ministry and campus crusade, leading the college students the right way, preparing them for their new job after graduation from college, telling them how to witness to their fellow student in the Campus, telling them how to work with other people in an office environment. especially people of all other religions.

The life of Jesus Christ in the life of believing Christians is a life of preaching, teaching sharing the knowledge of Jesus with other people of different cultures, ethnicities and people of all other races. The life of Jesus Christ is the life of love, a loving God with your whole heart, mind, spirit, soul and body, loving your neighbor as you love yourself. The life of Jesus Christ is the life of visiting the sick in the hospitals, praying for them; visiting the prisoners in the state and federal prisons and praying for them. Visit the senior citizens in the nursing homes, rehabilitation facilities, senior citizens' homes across the country and pray for them.

The life of Jesus Christ in the life of believers is the life of prayer, praying for the children in orphanage homes, foster homes and in their homes so that they can receive good care from those who are caring for them. The life of Jesus Christ in the life of believing Christians is the life of singing, the gospel songs, writing a drama play, helping the poor and the needy, sheltering the homeless, giving food, clothing to those who are in need of clothes, helping senior citizens to fix their broken homes, Christian counseling for the people who are in distress and oppressed, letting them know that Christ is all sufficient, all knowing, all powerful and he will fix their life and make it better in due time.

The life of Jesus Christ in the life of believing Christians is a life of prayer, praying for ourselves, our children, grandchildren, our relatives our friends, our coworkers, our church members, and most importantly, praying for our enemies; asking the Father for what we needed or for what we wanted to do, and for what we have done; praying for our food before we eat it, praying for our child from the womb before the baby is born and continuing our prayer without ceasing, praying for everything inside us and outside; pray quietly, pray aloud, pray in our room, pray in a public place if it is required or permitted by law. As Christians, we have straight access to the throne of grace through our Lord Jesus Christ. We can confidently, boldly pray for everything that is going on in the world, by praying for the nations and their governing rulers.

The life of Jesus Christ in the life of believing Christians is a life of thanksgiving, thanking the Father through our Lord Jesus Christ for what he has done, what he is doing and for what he is going to do, or doing presently in our lives. The life of Jesus Christ in the life of believing Christians is a life of blessing the Lord, praising his holy name every minute of our life. The life of Jesus Christ in the life of believing Christians is a life of rejoicing. Christians should rejoice that, their name is written in the book of life, in the book of the lamb and we are one in Christ as he and the rather are one. God knows our name. We have a straight, and unwavering faith that connected all Christians to the Father through his Son who is at his right hand whom all the authority in heaven and on earth has been given, Christ, and through Christ we have the authority to take the gospel of God to the end of the earth.

The life of Jesus Christ in the life of believing Christians cannot, and will never be, compared to any life on earth. It is the gift of grace of God to salvation that no money can buy; the gift of grace is free leading to eternal life in Jesus Christ. The life of Jesus Christ in the life of believing Christians is the life of the overcomer. In Christ, we overcome all forces of sources of evil that rise up against us, all the Satanic attacks, persecution, rejection, afflictions, tribulations, sickness, financial instabilities, problems, loss of loved ones by death, loss of jobs, educational problems, marriage problems and children's sicknesses in various ways. In Jesus Christ all the work of Satan is destroyed permanently in our lives, in all the areas of our lives, because he knows what we are going through and he has the power of the Holy Spirit to indwell all believing Christians to take care of all our problems.

The life of Jesus Christ in the life of believing Christians is the best life on earth, living on earth with the power of the heavenly host, the life to which the Spirit of God is connected, and controlled and directed with the love of God, which is in Jesus Christ our Lord. Let all those who know Christ and those who do not know him embrace the life of Jesus and live in him all the days of their life. It is a new life from this earth to heaven, a peaceable, peaceful and enjoyable life that God requires from all the people in the world.

"When the angels had left them and gone into heaven, the shepherds said to one another, 'Let's go to Bethlehem and see this thing that has happened, which the Lord has told us about" (Luke 2:15). The greatest blessing is that believing Christians will be able to see our Lord Jesus Christ face-to-face and believers will be ready when Christ comes to live forever on earth.

Pastoral Prayer for Christians

GOD THE FATHER ALMIGHTY OUR GRACIOUS FATHER, the Father of our Lord Jesus Christ the true Son of the Father full of grace and truth, the Holy Spirit, the counselor, the comforter, the Paraclate heavenly guest, I pray that you bless all the people in this world with your life, let them give their life to you and receive your life. You are the life changer, the restore, the provider, the maker of new creation. You are the Messiah who came to this world to save sinners and you are the friends of the sinners. You are the ever-living Lord: Father, Son and Holy spirit ever one God.

The abundant life that you have prepared for those who love you will never end. Open the hearts, minds, eyes, spirits, souls and bodies of all those who believe in you. Let them follow your word, your commandment. Let them be able to share your love and your life with many people who do not know you and let them be able to lead them to your gift of eternal life, which is only in you Christ Jesus. Let your Holy Spirit empower all the Christians in this world; let them be able to serve you faithfully and truthfully with the power of the Holy Spirit. Let your Spirit be manifest in their lives. Let them get closer and closer to you and at the end, live with you in heaven.

Lord Jesus Christ Our Lord and our Savior, our redeemer King, let the power of anointing of the Holy Spirit fall on all the missionaries who are in the mission's field. In your holy name with your life in them, help all Christians to be able to heal the sick, take the gospel good news message to the caves of the earth, villages, the wilderness, to the mountains. Through their witnessing to the sinners and the lost, let souls be worn into your holy hands in millions, and millions every day until the gospel of God reaches everyone and every inhabitant soul living on earth in their own language. Remember our Lord and Savior, you do not want anyone to perish; you want them to come to the knowledge of repentance and pray for forgiveness of sins, which is only in you our Lord.

Fulfill the great commission through all the Christians in the world. Let your feet be their feet, let your hands be their hands and help them to reach the unreachable. Let your light shine in the darkest part of this world. Let those who sit in the shadow of darkness see your light and follow your light and stay in your light forever. Help all the Christians to receive your life, to live your life, to live in you forever. Let all Christians know that the life of Jesus Christ in the life of Christians is the best and perfect life—a life that is connected to the Spirit of God, living with God from this earth to heaven. God the Father Almighty, the father of our Lord Jesus Christ, In Jesus Christ, matchless and great Holy name I pray. Amen, amen, amen.

"Simeon took him in his arms and praised God, saying: Sovereign Lord, as you have promised, you now dismiss your servant in peace. For my eyes have seen your salvation, which you have prepared in the sight of all people a light for revelation to the Gentiles and for glory to your people Israel. The child's father and mother marveled at what was said about him" (Luke 2:28-32). Scripture reveals that Simeon was an old man, whom the Lord God kept alive in order for him to see the glory and the salvation of God promised to men arrived to the world of sin.

Biblical Indexes

John 15:1-2, John, John 12:49-50, 15:5-6, John15:7, John 14:13, John 15:9-10, John 17:1-26, John 3:2, John 13: 13-14, John 14:26, John 15:1, John 15:5, John 15:12-14, John 20:21, John 4:50, John 14:15, John 14:4, John 17:15, John 1:29, John 5:39, John 15:5, John 6:37, John 20:22, John 4:7, John 4:19, John 4:22-26, John4:23, John4:29, John 4:4, John 4:13-14,John 10:5, John 10:11-16, John 14:6

Acts 3:16, Acts 1:9, Acts 2:1-4, Acts 1:4b-5,

Roman 8:5-10, Roman 6:20, Romans 5:5, Romans 3:21-22, Romans 8:9-10, Romans 8:33-34, Romans 3:24, Romans 8:23, Romans 14:17, Romans 5:1, Romans 8:35-39

1st Corinthians 10:13, 1st Corinthians 13:7, 1st Corinthians 15:52-54, 1st Corinthians 6:19-20

2nd Corinthians 5:17-19, 2nd Corinthians 5:17, 2nd Corinthians 5:17-20

Galatians 3:13, Galatians 2:20

Ephesians 3:17-19, Ephesians 3:16, Ephesians 3:30, Ephesians 1:7, Ephesians 1:14, Ephesians 2:4-6,

Philippians 2:10-11

Colossian 2:18, Colossians 3:4, Colossians 1:15-16, Colossians 3:1-2

2nd Thessalonians 1:12, 2nd Thessalonians 3:1,

1st Timothy 2:5-6, Timothy 4:10, 1st Timothy 1:17, 1st Timothy6:13-16,

2nd Timothy 2:3-4, Timothy 4:7-8

Titus 2:12

Hebrews 12:2-3, Hebrews 10:7-10, Hebrew 10:38, Hebrews 8:6, 9:15, Hebrews 12:24, Hebrews8:10, 13 , Hebrews 8:11, Hebrews 8:12, Hebrews 13:8, Hebrews 7:24, Hebrews 9:12, Hebrews 7:27, Hebrews 9:28, Hebrews 1:3, Hebrews 3:4-6, Hebrews 1:13, Hebrews 13:20

James 4:7-8

1ˢᵗ Peter 1:18-19, 1ˢᵗ Peter 1:15-16, 1ˢᵗ Peter 2:1-3, 1ˢᵗ Peter 2:1-2, 1ˢᵗ Peter2:5b, 1ˢᵗ Peter 2:7, 1ˢᵗ Peter 5:4

2ⁿᵈ Peter 3:18, 2ⁿᵈ Peter 1:11,

1ˢᵗ John 2:27, 1ˢᵗ John 1:9, 1ˢᵗ John 5:11-13

Jude: 25

Revelation 14:14

Bibliography

World Bible Dictionary Student Edition by Don Fleming

World Bible Publishers 1996

The Dead Sea Scrolls—Introduction to Biblical Archaeology November 1, 1997 Rose Publishing

The Complete Work of Flavius Josephus 1848 by Thomas Nelson

Christ's Resurrection in Early Christianity and the Making of New Testament by Markus Vinzent, Ashgate Publishing Company September, 2011

The Bible as History by Werner Keller Bantam—Publisher Nov.1, 1983

The Authentic Gospel of Jesus by Geza Vermes September 30, 2004 Pengun Publisher.

Expository Dictionary of Bible Words by Stephen D. Renn

Hendrickson Publishers 2005

Easton's Bible Dictionary by Matthew George

Packard Technologies—Publisher (March 18, 2009)

The History of The Church by Eusebius 1965 Dorset Press

Believer's Bible Commentary, William MacDonald Edited

By Arthur Farstad, 1995 Thomas Nelson Publishers

Nashville Atlanta, USA (1995).

Evangelical Dictionary of Biblical Theology, Edited by

Walter A. Elwell, 1996 by Baker Book House Company

Grand Rapids, Michigan, USA (1996).

The Holy Bible, In King James Version, Dugan Publishers, Inc., 1987 Gordonsville, Tennessee Printed in Colombia (1987).

The Student Bible, New Revised Standard

The Student Bible, New Revised Standard Version1994 by The Zondervan Corporation Published by Zondervan Grand Rapids, Michigan, USA (1994)

Exploring New Testament Ralph Earle Beacon Hill Press 1955

Student Study Bible NRSV Zondervan—Grand Rapids Michigan USA 1994

Hayes D. A. The Septic Gospel and Acts, New York: Methodist Book Concern, 1919. The Best Introduction to these four books of New Testament.

Hurter, A.M/ A. Pattern For Life. Philadelphia Westminster Press, 1953.

Morgan G. Campbell The Parables of the Kingdom, New York Fleming H. Revell Company 1907

Fission, Floyd. Origin of the Gospel New York Abingdon Press 1938

Godspeed, Edger J. An Introduction to New Testament, Chicago University of Chicago Press, 1937

Dana, H. E. Searching the Scriptures. Kansas City Central Seminary press, 1946

Books previously published by the author:
Grace Dola Balogun

Grace Religious Books Publishing & Distributors, Inc. New York

BE HOLY FOR I AM HOLY will help all the believing Christians to know that God is a Holy God, and he want us to be holy in all the things that we do. The book will help you to practice a holy life from this earth to heaven.

"Woe to me! I cried, I am ruined! For I am a man of unclean lips, and I live among people of unclean lips, and my eyes have seen the King, the Lord Almighty." he was so amaze and he screamed, and he realized that he was a sinner, he confessed, repent and was purified by one of the Seraphs who flew to him a live coal in his hand, which he had taken with tongs from the alter" (Isaiah 6:5-6). Christians must learn and know that God is holy; if they are to experience the manifest presence of the glory of God in their life. When prophet Isaiah saw the glory of God in the temple, he screamed and his life changed completely.

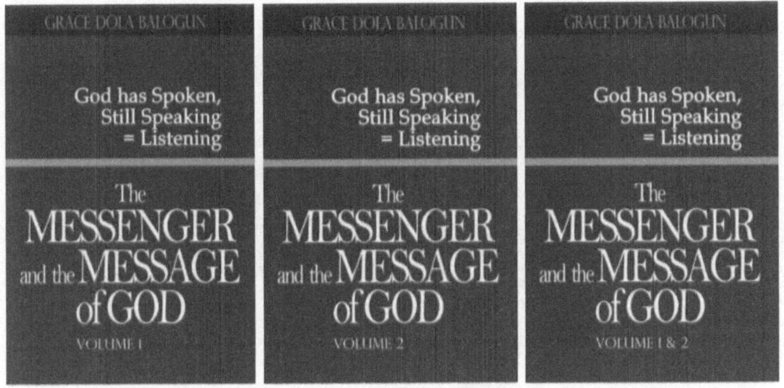

THE MESSENGER AND THE MESSAGE OF GOD—VOLUME 1, 2, 1 & 2

In the past, God communicated his Word, his Will through the prophets that he has chosen, qualified and anointed with the power of His Spirit to deliver his message to the King, and to the forefathers in the Old Testament. Jesus Christ called the disciples to follow him in His ministry as God the Father called all the prophets to deliver his message to the people in the Old Testament. Today, God has spoken and revealed himself to us by his Son Jesus Christ in a full complete message that transcends all previous words by God. God hath appointed him the heir of all things; by him God made the worlds, both visible and invisible, things in heaven and things on earth....

PRAYER THE SOURCE OF STRENGTH FOR LIFE —English Edition

Prayer the Source of Strength for Life is a powerful book that will energize your spirit to pray more and more until the prayer is part of your life and until the gate of Heaven is opened and your prayer is answered. Your prayer life will change your life.

LA ORACION FUENTE DE FORTALEZA PARA LA VIDA —Spanish Edition

Dios no's dio el poder de la oracion, quiere que lo usemos; debemos illamar, comunicarnos con el en todo lo que estemo spasando. El espera saber denosotros.

SPIRIT POWER VOLUMES I AND II

Spirit Power Volumes I and II both discuss the power of the Holy Spirit in the lives of believers. The power of the Spirit of God begins from the creation of the world until today. That power will also continue until Christ returns to reign. Hallelujah.

THE CROSS AND THE CRUCIFIXION

Our Lord Jesus Christ died on the cross to bring forth love and compassion. The impact of sins on human life brings all other evil into our world, from one society to another society, from one culture to another. But in Christ, we are clothed with His holiness. We have the gift of eternal life. The gate of Heaven is open and we are eligible for our inheritance in Heaven. Hallelujah! Hosanna in the Highest. Jesus Christ paid it all, unto Him all we owe. The cross of Christ is the cross of joy, peace, and righteousness to all who believe in Him.

THREE SIMPLE SOLUTIONS FOR WORLD PEACE

Three Simple Solutions for World Peace is a book that clears all the confusion that many people of the world have been going through for many years. It is a book that gives light and advice to some of the problems that plague the world, and that offers solutions for these problems. It is a book that is full of knowledge, understanding and solutions that will bring some peace to the world.

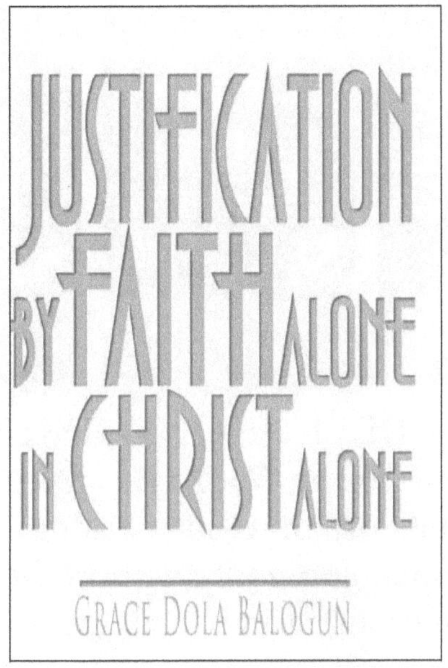

JUSTIFICATION BY FAITH ALONE IN CHRIST ALONE

Justification by Faith Alone in Christ Alone will clear all the confusion of believers' faith in Jesus Christ. Believers will also rejoice in the long-sufferings—they will rejoice in their sufferings, afflictions, persecutions, rejections and all various trials that may press in on them because these long-sufferings will help all of the believers to be redeemed in Christ.

CHRISTIAN CELL PHONE SERIES:

Christian Cell Phone Godly Wisdom helps readers understand the role of God's wisdom and the importance of obtaining godly wisdom in one's life to produce prosperous results in all areas of life. These areas are critical and include family, relationships and finances. The acquiring of God's wisdom is to be sought after in life and will affect others as well.

Christian Cell Phone God's Favor is designed to give readers knowledge of God's favor from the Old Testament to the New Testament. With an analysis of the favor that was on Jesus, the Son of God, the reader will find that God's favor can completely change one's life and lead others to Christ as well.

Christian Cell Phone God's Anointing is an examination of the anointing on the life of Jesus that includes present day believers in Christ Jesus. This anointing can be applied to all areas of life and can be seen in miraculous ways. The anointing is what makes our life incredible and supernatural, drawing all of those who see, to Christ.

JESUS CHRIST THE JOY OF CHRISTMAS

Jesus Christ the Joy of Christmas gives praise and tribute to the child who was born in Bethlehem. Tracing the prophecies of Old about this King that was born, the author gives an account of the sinless Lamb of God who came to take away the peoples' sins from a biblical perspective, who is the real Joy of Christmas.

PRAYER FOR THE BULLY VICTIMS AND THE BULLY TOO!

Prayer for the Bully Victims and the Bully Too addresses the issue of the bully from the classroom to the home. By the use of scriptural application, the author looks at what can be done to help the bully kid and their victims. The author has written several key prayers that readers can use to help either the bully victim or parents who are dealing with a child who has become a bully.

I AM THE RESURRECTION AND THE LIFE

I Am The Resurrection and The Life: Powerful, inspirational and written from a firm biblical perspective, multi-published author Grace Dola Balogun, gives life to others through the power of Jesus Christ who is the resurrection and the life. This book will open eyes to the amazing and abundant blessings of accepting Jesus Christ as your Lord and Savior, giving keen insight into the Scriptures on the power available to all through the Holy Spirit with an emphasis on aspects of eternal life for the believer.

I AM THE ETERNAL LIFE

I Am The Eternal Life: Encouraging, uplifting and filled with a sound biblical perspective, this book encourages believers and non-believers alike to look to the One that is Jesus Christ, the Son of God, who is the bread of life and the one who gives eternal life to all who believe in Him. This book gives readers a heavenly perspective on their life, revealing believer's God-given destiny and purpose to all who call on Jesus Christ as their Lord and Savior. The truth of the Gospel and the Good News is eloquently displayed in this delightful and insightful read.

HE WHO BELIEVES IN ME SHALL NEVER DIE

He Who Believes In Me Shall Never is a fascinating teaching, revealing Jesus as the way, the truth and the life—the everlasting life. All who believe in Him shall never die. Beginning from the Old Testament, the author looks at the fall of humanity through the sin of disobedience through Adam and Eve. Comparing this fall to the sin of disobedience today, the author reveals scriptural truths in the lives of Enoch, Elijah and Moses. The author gives insight into the baptism of the Holy Spirit and gives examples of the Spirit's power and the purpose for which the power is given to believers. The author has given key scriptural insights that all who believe in Jesus Christ will have everlasting life in Him that continues to Heaven.

FORGIVE OUR DEBTS AS WE FORGIVE OUR DEBTORS

Forgive our Debts as we Forgive our Debtors speaks of divine forgiveness from the Lord and the Lord's commandment to forgive others, including ourselves. With the Lord's Prayer as a foundation, author Grace D. Balogun, explores from the Old Testament to the New Testament meanings of forgiveness and the consequences of sin. The author gives keen biblical insight into the subject of forgiveness, bringing life-changing healing that is only acquired through the power of forgiveness.

SHE MUST BE SILENT: THE GREAT COMMISSION BESTOWED ON BOTH MEN AND WOMEN is a controversial book that takes a look at the role of women throughout biblical history and gives key scriptural insight into the role of women from the Old Testament to the New Testament. An encouraging, enlightening read, this book is recommended for women and men who want to understand the role of women from a biblical perspective. This book does an excellent job in giving insight into key roles that women play in God's redemptive plan and sheds light on the empowerment of the Holy Spirit that is given to both men and women by God, who is no respecter of persons.

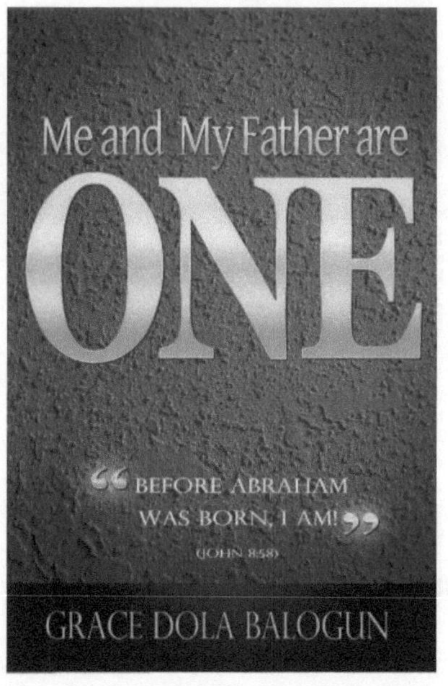

ME AND MY FATHER ARE ONE: BEFORE ABRAHAM WAS BORN, I AM *(John 8:58)* explains that God the Father and Jesus Christ are one from the beginning. In this book, the reader will learn that the plan of redemption is from the Father and is carried out through His Son, Jesus Christ, who is the Word of God. In the beginning, before Abraham, before Adam and Eve, Christ says, "I Am." Written from a biblical perspective, the author displays that Jesus Christ was in the beginning and as Scripture says, "He is before all things, and in him all things hold together" (Colossians 1:17).

About The Author

Grace Dola Balogun graduated from Fordham University Graduate School of Religion and Religious Education in the year 2010 with an M.A. in Religion and Religious Education. She has been a prayer mentor and advisor for many Christians of all denominations for many years.

Visit her online at:
www.Gracereligiousbookspublishers.com
Grace's Blog:
http://author-grace-dola-balogun.blogspot.com/
Facebook:
https://www.facebook.com/grace.d.balogun
Twitter:
https://twitter.com/prayersource

To order additional copies of this book, please email: info@gracereligiousbookspublishers.com.
This book may also be ordered from 30,000 wholesalers, retailers and booksellers in the U. S., and in Canada and over 100 countries globally.

To contact Grace Dola Balogun for an interview or a speaking engagement, please e-mail: info@gracereligiousbookspublishers.com

The Spirit and the bride say, "Come!" And let the one who hears say, "Come!" Let the one who is thirsty come; and let the one who wishes take the free gift of the water of life (Revelation 22:17).
MARANATHA EVEN SO COME LORD JESUS (1ST CORINTHIANS 16:22, REVELATION 22:20).

ORDER FORM
TO ORDER YOUR COPY OF ANY BOOK:
NAME:______________________________________

ADDRESS:_________________________________

TELEPHONE:_____________________________

FAX#:____________________________________

MAIL:____________________________________

QUANTITY:_______________________________

MAIL TO:_________________________________

**Grace Religious Books Publishing &
Distributors, Inc. New York
213 Bennett Avenue
New York, NY 10040**